From the Bottom Up

Winner of
THE FLANNERY O'CONNOR AWARD
FOR SHORT FICTION

From the Bottom Up

Stories by Leigh Allison Wilson

The University of Georgia Press
Athens

Set in Linotron Baskerville
The paper in this book meets the guidelines for
permanence and durability of the Committee on
Production Guidelines for Book Longevity of the
Council on Library Resources.

Printed in the United States of America

Library of Congress Cataloging in Publication Data

Wilson, Leigh Allison.
    From the bottom up.

    Contents: From the bottom up—Mildred Motley
and the son of a bitch—The raising—[etc.]
    I. Title.
PS3573.I459F7   1983   813'.54   82–15975
ISBN 0–8203–0647–9

Grateful acknowledgment is given to the maga-
zines in which several of the stories in this collec-
tion first appeared. "Invictus" appeared in *The
Southern Review* (Spring 1979), "Broken Mirrors" in
Mademoiselle (October 1979), "Mildred Motley and
the Son of a Bitch" in *Skyline* (Winter 1981), and
"From the Bottom Up" in *The Georgia Review*
(Spring 1981).

For my mother

GLENDA FRANKLIN BLACKBURN

and my father

HOWARD LEE WILSON

1933–1982

I said to the man who was appointed to wash him—would that he
had yielded obedience to my counsel,—
Put away from him the water, and wash him with the tears of
honour, shed in lamentation for him:
And remove these fragrant substances collected for his corpse,
and perfume him rather with the odours of praise;
And order the noble angels to carry him, in honour. Dost thou not
behold them attending him?
Cause not men's necks to be strained by bearing him: enough
are they laden already by his benefits.

from "The Story of Noor-ed Deen"
The Thousand and One Nights

Contents

From the Bottom Up

Old Blackburn's granddaughter, Lorraine, sat on the edge of the bathtub and thumped the heels of her patent-leather shoes against the porcelain sides. Her legs hung like sapling trunks below where her dress hiked up crooked at the waist, and she was busy picking strings from the cotton hem. The morning sun splayed through the bathroom window, caught the reflection of Old Blackburn full in the face while he knotted his tie in the medicine-cabinet mirror, and beveled from the glass onto his granddaughter as if to enlighten them according to age. Swinging the mirror a little allowed Old Blackburn both to knot his tie and, squinting, to watch the child as she pulled little irreparable cockades in the material of her dress. She pulled a six-inch string, staring intently as the cotton writhed up onto her thigh. Then she dropped the thread to the tile floor, where several others already lay curled.

Old Blackburn practiced a benevolent smile in the mirror, baring his teeth; his nose dropped like a boll of cotton and the lines of the smile split his jaw like a field furrow. When she left for Nashville all Ella Ray had said was "Just don't beat her to death," and from that minute on that's practically all he'd wanted to do. He stopped practicing. He liked to tell relatives that he received the aquiline features in the family, that he was the product of a buried strain of nobility on his father's side; and with the world falling apart from the bottom on upward, Old Blackburn saw no reason for the noble to smile.

"Are you ready to go?" he said and noticed that his nose was indeed as stern and proud as an eagle's. It seemed to ripple in flight through the dazzle of reflected sunlight. "Are you ready to go?"

"We got showers in Knoxville," Lorraine said. "We don't have no bathtubs. Momma says they carry disease in the shape of spiders." She leaned over and stuck her head in the bathtub and made mewing noises. "Says they carry gangrene." She dipped and slid over the lip of the bathtub, mewing. On the back of her dress two streaks of dull green met in the shape of a great bird flying across the cotton.

"Have you sat in something?"

"I thought I saw a rat," Lorraine said, her voice resounding in the hollows of the tub. "They breed rats in Knoxville, in the sewers where every time you flush . . . "

"What have you sat in, girl?"

". . . You're feeding a rat," she said.

Old Blackburn picked his coat off a hanger on the back of the bathroom door and held it by the collar as if to wipe his hands on the black polyester. In the mirror he noted the gravity of his aspect, the sharp slash of black tie against white collar, the proud nose above the slit of an unvacillating mouth, riveting green eyes that blinked but never connived or winked. He thought himself the picture of restrained nobility, a last bastion of human dignity. DEATH WITH DIGNITY was the motto of the funeral home and, though he didn't own it, still Old Blackburn drove the hearse, consoled the bereaved with words of unsentimental wisdom, and helped carry the coffin from hearse to grave-site, all the while inspiring the confidence of mourners and gravediggers alike with his calm severity. Old Blackburn was indispensable to the many dignified deaths administered by the Jefferson Funeral Home, and today would crown his achievement. Today they would bury Thomas P. Appleton, former mayor of Jefferson City and beloved owner of Appleton's Drugs, a chain of drugstores that linked half of the state with pharmaceuticals. And half the state would be at the cemetery to watch Old Blackburn drive the hearse slowly forward, parting whole clusters of weeping women and dour-faced men, to stare with not a little relief as he stepped proudly and vigorously from the hearse, his black and white appearance tracing a fine figure under the noon sun. His whole person would scream DEATH WITH DIGNITY to the awaiting crowds.

"Lorraine, sit up and listen to me," he said and shut the medicine cabinet. The sunlight had shifted, had fallen into one pure stream of yellow that flooded the back of Lorraine's head and formed a frowzy halo. "You will take off your dress and put on another. You will do it in five minutes and will do nothing to mess it once you've dressed. Do you hear me?"

"I ain't done nothing but listen since I got here. There ain't nothing to do *but* talk and listen when you're in the middle of nowhere. We got TV in Knoxville."

"Television is the eye of little people, and little people are tearing the world into little pieces. It's an evil, Lorraine, the eye of evil." Lorraine puckered her lips and pulled another string from her dress, her eyes set vacantly toward the door of the bathroom as if in wary contemplation of escape. "You will right now go change your dress. The funeral starts in an hour."

"I reckon he won't mind if we're a little late," she said, snickering into her sleeve, then wiping her mouth on the cotton. "I reckon he can sit tight for a while." She stood up, her dress twisted sideways at the waist, and pranced out of the bathroom.

"I'm no baby-sitter," Old Blackburn had said to Ella Ray when she dropped Lorraine off without asking either his permission or his consent, "and I'm no kindergarten service neither."

Ella Ray had just stood there, dabbing pink lipstick on her mouth and champing down on a pink-dappled Kleenex while Lorraine roamed around his living room, inspecting his collection of glass elephant pieces, grabbing them up and staring them right between the eyes with a look of malice on her face. "What am I supposed to do around here?" Lorraine said and Ella Ray said, "Shut your mouth and sit down, please ma'am," and then Old Blackburn wagged his head back and forth, watching a glass elephant disappear in the palm of Lorraine's hand and reappear in little fractions on the wooden slats of the floor. It had taken her three minutes to shatter his piece.

"Papa, it's my chance in a lifetime," Ella Ray said and looked down at the slivers of glass. "I'm the only representative for Knox County in the whole Tennessee convention. Here's her suitcase. I really appreciate it, Papa." She showed Old Blackburn all of her front teeth and two of them bled a faint pink, then she squinted her eyes at Lorraine, saying "I'll wring your neck when I come back. Just remember that." Before he could move, Ella Ray was rushing out the front door and waving goodbye; "Just don't beat her to death" trailed after her like a flourish of trumpets, then she submerged into her car and left.

"Will this do?" Lorraine asked. She held the sides of her hem in both hands so that two wings of dark blue material formed under her arms. Flapping her wings she followed Old Blackburn down the hall and into the living room where she let go of the dress and flopped onto a couch, lying stomach-down on the cushions with her arms pointed toward an armrest.

"Up up and away," she said.

"Sit up and be quiet," Old Blackburn said. He pulled on his coat. Even though the cuffs of his shirt hung down two inches below the line of his coat sleeves, giving the appearance of broad white grins on his wrists, the polyester of both was spotless, unfrayed. Old Blackburn conjured an image of a proud but wise country preacher and thought for a second that perhaps he had missed his calling. "Sit up, we have to hurry. There's hundreds of people waiting for us."

He stood by a brown coffee table and picked up his wallet, placing it in the back left pocket of his trousers; then he picked up a set of keys, placing them in the front right pocket; then he picked up a store-bought carnation and planted it in the buttonhole of his lapel. If he had been a preacher, instead of rooting after line leakage for Western Union, he might still be preaching. They made him retire although he had more than once offered his services indefinitely; they gave him a silver watch that broke two weeks later and they sent him home. Every month he got a check from the state headquarters and enclosed with it, every six months or so, was a note that said "We miss you down here, you old rascal" or else "Come see us sometime." But the funeral home picked up on him as soon as he walked in the door—"Maybe we could use a good man like you," Mr. Toad had said. And Old Blackburn strode right into the job with the air of an incumbent governor, telling everybody that he worked for no pay, that money was nothing to a noble man.

"Sit up, sit down," Lorraine said, sitting up, "shut up, get dressed, listen to this, listen to that—I may's well be a hearing aid."

"You should thank God you're not worse off. There's people in the world without the legs to stand on." Old Blackburn walked to the front door, opened it, and stood there while Lorraine got up from the couch, her face inscrutably pinched around the eyes, and followed him outside. He locked the door, then put the keys back in his pocket.

"Dear Lord," she said. "Now I lay me down to sleep and if I should die before I wake, I pray You Lord to take take take." With a look of surprise she giggled. "Take take take," she said again and skipped down the porch steps.

"You better watch your mouth, miss. People are struck dead every day." If he had been a preacher, he could have saved Lorraine's soul, hundreds of souls, and abruptly he pictured himself leading great masses of black-robed people into the cleansing waters of a beautiful blue river. He would preach that God helps those that help themselves, that He takes only the great and noble unto Him—no little people—that the Lord giveth and the Lord taketh away. His words would move grown men to tears, and they would follow him out of the rabble and rabidity into the path of a severe dignity.

Lorraine hung on the open door of his Pontiac, rocking it back and forth on the tip of her toes. Beside the car Old Blackburn cocked his hand in a salute, warding off the sunlight, and inspected the weather way off past his neighborhood tract, past the fields of half-grown tobacco, way off to where the mountains crouched against an encroaching wall of black clouds. They were swelled to rupturing, moving in quickly from the northeast; there might be rain on the funeral. He inspected his house to make sure the storm windows were all shut. It was pink brick. Every house in the tract was pink brick, although the front doors and windows got shuffled around from house to house, making the row of them look like one face strung in a variety of emotional positions. Old Blackburn's house was in a state of astonishment: two gaping windows stared over a wide front door that gaped ever so slightly outward. At last he got into the car and revved the engine, satisfied that all his windows were tight against the rain. Lorraine climbed in beside him and immediately turned on the radio. Old Blackburn turned it off.

"I reckon the radio's a evil, too," she said and folded her arms, looking out her window with a stiff neck. Sunlight streamed in through the front window and formed tiny dull pockets of gold dust on the dashboard. When Old Blackburn backed the car slowly out of the driveway the light veered and struck the front of Lorraine's head, making her hair turn into a glowing nimbus, while he manipulated the wheel in a dim gray shade, his back reared erect against the seat. He drove with a grim authority, the whole car seeming to extend and shape itself under his direction. A mail-order black man in riding britches stood at the end of his driveway and pointed toward the garage with a black crop.

"He looks bored," Lorraine said, letting her neck go loose. She was approximately the same height as the statue. "He looks like his arm's tired." They drove out of the tract, turned onto the main highway, and set off through the farmsteads and the tenant houses with their grubby, spidery children crouched in front on the packed dirt, and on past a shuttered Esso station and a sunken brown barn that had SEE ROCK CITY painted in white on the roof. Lorraine sat and swiveled her head left and right, her eyes flicking over the landscape. Old Blackburn sat as rigid as an ancient boulder.

"I seen a movie just like this," she said. "They had soldiers come and burn it all down."

"I want you to be quiet when we get to the funeral home," he said, "and I want you to stay beside me the whole time." He sat so stiffly that his mouth seemed to be the only movable part, and it moved with a sparse pecking action across the jaw. "There's hundreds of people at the cemetery and you might get lost. You're liable to get taken home by mistake."

"They spared the women and children, though. Took them to the city and put them in the sewers to scrub for the rest of their lives. I seen it on the late show."

Up ahead was a gray stoplight, lined on both sides by clusters of scraggly old buildings. Off in the distance the road continued on into more farmsteads and tenant houses, the pavement cutting a clean arrow through the yellow-green landscape, pointing straight into the welling pregnancy of thunderclouds that were shoved head and belly over the mountains. Old Blackburn turned left at the stoplight, then drove into the parking lot of the funeral home. Except for the modern wing on the south side, the funeral home had a colonial facade and could have been the house of an old and rich and decorous family; the hearses lined up in the lot could have been a fleet of limousines; and the well-dressed undertakers who lounged on the front veranda might have been the family's prodigal sons, lazing away the morning in the coolness of the shade.

For years the policy of the funeral home had been to assemble the parties of the bereaved at the cemetery, then to deliver the coffin immediately before the service began. They maintained that a funeral procession was an indignity to the dead, that it sullied the respectability of the funeral for ignorant or derisive or impassive spectators to watch the mourners drive through town. And Old Blackburn maintained, in private, that it kept the bereaved from wandering aimlessly around the home, impeding an orderly execution of their affairs. More than any other place he had ever frequented, he felt at home here. It was dignified.

"Nice place you got here," Lorraine said and got out of the car. She stood with her arms planted on her waist and looked up at the wrought-iron DEATH WITH DIGNITY sign over the entrance. Little chips of black paint had fallen off it, revealing patches of pale gray between the letters.

"It says 'Death with Dignity,'" Old Blackburn said. "It means we're careful here."

"I can read it. I been reading for a million years," Lorraine said. "Just about exactly a million years." He headed toward the glass door under the sign and held it open for Lorraine, but she hung back, adjusting her dress, then rubbing her nose with two pronged fingers, then craning her neck backwards with her eyes rolled up in her head.

"Does it stink in there?" she asked, her voice catching as a roll of thunder sounded in the distance, resounded against the home, and drifted off into the air.

"Get in here, Lorraine," Old Blackburn said and kept his form as rigid as a well-dressed scarecrow. "If you keep your mouth shut in here maybe they'll think you've got good sense."

"Maybe it's them that's without the sense," Lorraine said. "They're the ones that live in this one-horse town, not me." Snorting, she marched through the door and into the home. Old Blackburn let the door shut by itself behind them and looked over Lorraine's head up the corridor where the gravediggers usually leaned on the walls and spat on the floor and passed around hand-rolled cigarettes that slashed between their lips while they spoke. But there wasn't a soul in the corridor today except for a single black man in overalls who was sweeping the floor at a slow lope. At each step he thrust his head forward, gave the floor a swipe, then retracted his neck, swiping and thrusting and retracting as if any minute he might uncover something of value on the floor. Old Blackburn stood in the middle of his path with his shoulders squared to show he was a man with a mission.

"Where's Mr. Toad, young man?" he asked, pecking the words.

"Mought be downstairs, Blackburn," the man said and continued sweeping. A spray of dust billowed over Old Blackburn's shoes but the man kept sweeping and stabbing his neck as though stuck in neutral in front of a stoplight. "Mought be upstairs and mought be on the porch. Mought be at home with dinner on the table. Don't know."

"You should get a vacuum cleaner," Lorraine told the man. "One of them with the long cords. They'll suck up anything."

"Is that right," the man said and looked at her. "Need me a swimming pool too, and a goose that lays the golden eggs." He tapped the broom on Old Blackburn's feet until he stepped aside. Then, shifting gears, he went loping on down the hall behind the broom.

"If you weren't so ignorant," Old Blackburn said, stamping his shoes, "I'd think you were touched in the head. He don't need you to tell him what to do." She turned her back to him and looked at the wall, her shoulders drawn up in a little blue square.

"Blackburn!" a thin voice said, preceding a short, thin man in a black suit. It was Mr. Toad, teetering down the corridor with his right hand wiping his face with a white handkerchief. "I want to have a word with you, Blackburn." Old Blackburn drew himself up to his full presence and stood ready for orders.

"Listen, I'm in a hurry. You've got number two today and the funeral starts in thirty minutes." He wiped his face, although tiny globules of sweat popped out on his brow like indelible pink bubbles after each swipe, and he stared at the carnation on Old Blackburn's chest.

"And the other thing, Blackburn: we've been, well, we've been getting complaints about you. I believe this will be your last day with us."

"What do you mean?" Old Blackburn said and squinted his eyes to get Mr. Toad in better focus.

"I mean we've had complaints, attacks even, from the Devotie party. They say you were morbid to them, that you told Mrs. Devotie that her husband was better off dead than alive, that he was deader alive than buried. I can't have my men disrespecting the clients. You've got thirty minutes, I tell you." Mr. Toad turned on his heel and started teetering away, his handkerchief pressed to his face like a giant baby's breath

"Number two," he said over his shoulder, and then he disappeared.

"Number two," Old Blackburn said, still squinting for focus. The whole hallway seemed to be losing its shape, to be drifting in soft pieces away from the center. But there were still the funeral and the hundreds of people and the hearse with him in it that would part the sea of faceless mourners and his clean, stern black and white appearance. The hallway came together again and in the middle of it stood Lorraine. As soon as he focused her into the picture she turned sideways, standing there with her arms hanging down close to her sides.

"We've got thirty minutes," he said. "Number two."

Lorraine shrugged her shoulders and stayed put.

"It's the number two is what we've got," he said and walked down the hall toward the door. Opening the glass Old Blackburn glanced behind him, saw Lorraine following him at seven paces with her eyes hooded and sullen, then he walked out into the parking lot. He got into the number two hearse and waited until Lorraine got in beside him, head turned toward the window, neck stiff, arms pulled toward the car door. It started to rain, angry sheets followed by tentative patters followed by a steady dull hiss, and he turned on the wipers, watching the windshield go from confusion to half-circled clarity. Pulling in a deep breath that seemed to tighten his back and hold it at attention, Old Blackburn started the engine and pulled out of the parking lot. Except for the coffin proper the whole interior of the hearse was chalk-white leather that gave off a fluorescent glow and illuminated the driving area with a silver tarnish.

"Hundreds of people," Old Blackburn said, "hundreds and hundreds of people," and then, as if his brain had stuck on a difficult problem, he said "Hunnerds and hunnerds a people" a little louder.

They drove into the cemetery, rounded a curve. There, at the bottom of a sloping hill, he could see a tremendous circus tent that seemed to bulge with people, all dressed in black. They swelled past the sides of the tent and strung out across the lawn, dark umbrellas blooming over every head, television cameras rolling here and there in the crowd. Old Blackburn felt something like an intoxicating pride seep into every cranny of his person, felt his muscles tighten and rear back, felt his clothes starch up and grow powerful to see. Guiding the hearse into the outskirts of the shaded people, he kept a look of solidity on his face, his eyes and nose and mouth as stern and proud as stone, glancing only once at Lorraine, silent and unmoving against the door.

An umbrella and the black trousers of a fat man disengaged from the crowd and trotted up to the hearse. The man tapped on Old Blackburn's window with a notebook until he rolled it down.

"We have arrived," Old Blackburn said, solemnly.

"No you ain't," the fat man said and adjusted his umbrella, then pursed his fat lips at the notebook. "The number two party is down the hill. This is the Appleton party, number one."

"But this is my funeral!" Old Blackburn shouted.

"Down the hill and hurry for God's sake, it's raining." Then the umbrella and the fat legs eased back into the shifting, thronging welter of umbrellas and legs. Old Blackburn stared at the drops of water that came through the open window and stained his shoulder. He put his hand on them making a patch of wetness spread onto his coat sleeve, and he studied it as if it were a scientific experiment. With a little gurgling sound coming out of the pit of his stomach he put the hearse in reverse and backed down the hill all the way to where a little awning covered a small group: four men and three women beside a square hole in the ground. He stopped the hearse beside the awning. The four men opened the back of the hearse and carried the coffin over to the hole, the rain making perverse tears gush down on their grim faces. Still gurgling, Old Blackburn opened his door and got out and stood with his head bared to the rain.

"My own flesh and blood," one woman wailed and her voice drowned through the rushing rain. "My own flesh and blood."

"Hunnerds," Old Blackburn said. The rain was blinding him, and he felt his knees, his back, grow very tired, wanting to return to the ground. A vision of a broken watch loomed before his eyes and behind that telegraph poles stretched on and on, toppling abruptly into a beautiful blue river where robed bodies floated face-down, hundreds and hundreds of bodies. But he wasn't even in the picture. The gurgling sound grew to a mighty surge down the base of his spine, prickly as broom straw, and he crouched on the grass to stop the flow. The funeral began in front of him but he couldn't see it and, blind, he groped around on the grass for something to hold on to.

"Let's get out of here, let's go home." Old Blackburn tried to focus his eyes and at last he could make out Lorraine in front of him, standing with her feet planted firmly on the grass. Between her white legs lay his carnation, mud-smeared, its stem stuck straight in the air. "Please, Papaw, let's go home." He held out his hand, groping, the world flashing in and out of focus, and she took it, suddenly looming gigantic before him, and pulled him to his feet.

"Flesh and blood," he said, as if fetching for a forgotten lyric. Lorraine held his hand and tugged him toward the hearse.

"Let's go home," she said. "It's no one here to cry over." And Old Blackburn let her lead him like a child into the hearse, into that white interior, into that place where the dead were dignified.

"Home," Lorraine said.

"Flesh and blood," he repeated, tentatively.

He was just beginning to mourn.

Mildred Motley
and the Son of a Bitch

There were three things Mildred Motley Plonk needed: a decent man, a fortune, and a son of a bitch to kill. Already that day she had taken aim with a shotgun, pulled the trigger, and blown the heads off the milkman, the mailman, and the meter reader while they went about their business, never knowing the difference. She was looking forward—knees tucked against her porch railing, hands in her lap and lumped together like chitlins, eyes pointed toward the front yard—looking forward to killing the parcel post man when he came at three o'clock with a package from her brother, Kenneth Lee. In that package would be a pair of shoes (tennis shoes, green with broken laces), three packs of Juicy Fruit chewing gum (one pack already opened, its mouth gaping red and yellow, two pieces missing), and a paregoric for some bowel trouble she'd been having. Also in the package, on top of everything and edged with black lines, would be a note that explained what dose of paregoric to take so that she didn't stove up and reverse her needs.

Mildred Motley was not a psychic though, could not read minds or predict futures or raise the dead (except that she could make the jack of hearts flicker in and out between the deck of cards as if it had a will of its own, or as if she had a knack for that particular face card), couldn't even see through dense objects; Mildred Motley just knew her brother very well. She had killed Kenneth Lee, via the postal service, sixteen times and planned to keep killing him till he died of natural causes.

Now Mildred Motley was looking at her front yard. She could see the grass, overgrown but tidy, tall but cut clean at the top like a currycomb, and beyond that a spreading field of tobacco, and still farther the cusp of the Smoky Mountains, poking up above crinkled green tobacco stalks. From time to time Mildred Motley liked to pretend the mountains were an undulating serpent, that at some point, maybe next week, or at least in her lifetime, it would ripple upward and writhe belly-long over the whole of East Tennessee, slashing its tail across North Carolina and sinking its teeth into Georgia, particularly the city of Atlanta. Right now, though, they looked like mountains. To the left, two hundred yards beyond her own house, was another house, identical to hers but slightly enlarged and encased by a line of poplar trees; the poplars mingled their leaves and cloaked the whitewashed wood, the white fluttering through the green in little patches. Mildred Motley figured that something sinful went on in that house, it must, because no decent house would dress in trees then expose itself, slyly, when the wind blew. For years, six to be exact, she had destroyed that house and everyone in it—usually by fire, sometimes by flood—and once a month she borrowed a cup of sugar.

It reminded Mildred Motley of her grandfather, that house, the way it intimated indecent secrets, the way it flashed white entrails through loose clothing. Once her grandfather exposed himself to a nine-year-old girl who, though a little repulsed, took a keen interest in the sight (he said) and followed him around for eight years until he finally married her. But eventually her grandmother died—compensation, Mildred Motley thought, for her keen interest—and they buried her ashes in the family plot, then her grandfather went home and broke all of the pictures in the old house with a fire poker while Mildred Motley stared stupidly from a dark corner. She had been only six and could think of nothing else to do but chew the skin around her fingernails and stare, stupidly. Afterwards he drank all of her grandmother's toilet water, than laid up in his bedroom for two weeks, trying to die. The family had fights downstairs, each in turn claiming the furniture, the rugs, the house itself, until at last her grandfather pitched down the stairs and broke her Uncle Babcock's shoulder in one blow with the poker, ridding the house of them all.

"Crazy!" Uncle Babcock had cried. "Son of a bitch's crazy. Put him away, that's what, put the crazy bastard away."

"Missed his head by mere inches," her grandfather said, a long-stemmed cigarette careening at his lips. "But, and this ain't no lie, but that bastard still hung like a bloodsucker to Evelyn's tapestry rug. Arm broke and all! Tried to drag it out the front door and would've, by God, he would've if it weren't for me crippling him."

Mildred Motley squinted her eyes, eased the butts of her knees between the slats of the porch railing, and squinted into the grass of her lawn. A neighbor boy, a scrawny kid with plastic-frame glasses and acne mottles on his chin, cheeks, and forehead, an ugly kid, was supposed to cut the grass once a week, but he forgot last week and now the lawn lapped over the roots of her maple trees and rippled like pond water all the way to where the road came through. Still squinting, Mildred Motley placed the boy in the middle of the grass, let him cut his hair that was much too long, and shot him neatly through the heart. Then she put him back on his feet and made him mow her grass for free. After he finished she invited him up to the porch where she served up a glass of pink lemonade, the glass so cold it oozed tears down the sides. He emptied the glass, swallowing even the droplets of sweat that fell off his nose into the lemonade, then asked for more, his glasses askew at the nose and eyes.

"Take what you can get," Mildred Motley said and closed her eyes. Eight years ago, when she was eighteen, a late summer tornado had come groping through the hills, plunging down at random and snatching whole houses into the sky: parts of houses actually, she remembered, but the picture of an entire two-story house leaping skyward tickled the insides of her head, made her happy. Like a bolt from the blue, like a shot in the dark, even like a bat out of hell, the tornado appeared on the horizon of a cornfield where Mildred Motley was picking cornbores and squeezing them between her thumb and first finger. She wheeled around and ran down a row of corn, stumbling across stubbles and dirt clods, feeling the flat palms of corn leaves smack her in the face, on the arms, running until she got to a bomb shelter her father had built ("In case of a Red threat," he said) and then she was saved. Immediately John Henry, a farm hand, barged into the shelter after her, his cheeks puffed and jerking, his eyes like clods of dirt, bulging and brown. He slammed the metal door and leaned against it with his face working to straighten itself out.

"Mother of God," he said, body bent sideways, "Holy Mother of God."

Mildred Motley, though, was in control.

"Saw a tornado once," she said, "and it dug a trench six feet in the ground. Didn't let up till every body in Fairlawn Park sat on top of its headstone."

John Henry slid his backbone along the door until his bottom settled onto the concrete. He pressed his hands against the floor, holding it down, and the sound of freight trains rattled above them. Mildred Motley wiped cornbore guts onto the thighs of her bluejeans. The shelter was an empty ten-by-ten foot square of concrete that had little stress fissures running down its sides, and Mildred Motley wondered what an atom bomb would do to the little fissures.

"Knew a man that ended up in New York State because of a tornado," she said and looked at John Henry.

"Why don't you just shut up?" John Henry said, his face already straightening out. "Why don't you just shut the hell up?"

"Ended up in a tree near Albany. I heard he finally settled there."

John Henry snorted through his nose and Mildred Motley took a turn around the shelter. By the time she ended up back at John Henry's feet (they shot out of his pant legs and pointed toward the wall opposite the door), the sound of the tornado had turned into a troop of infantrymen marching above them, and by the time John Henry got to his feet, the sound was just a John Deere tractor groaning to a start.

"Looks like we'll live," she said, but John Henry was looking at her in a peculiar way, looking as if he wanted to shake her hand.

"Hee, hee," he said. "Hee, hee, hee."

"What's wrong with you?"

"Hee, hee, hee." John Henry unleashed the bib of his overalls in a flick with both hands. "Hee!"

"Hold on, hey, you crazy or what?"

"I take what I can get," he said and then his pants were around his ankles and he was stepping out of them. Mildred Motley felt the tips of her fingers grow stiff. Quick as a trigger she kicked John Henry with the point of her shoe and he spraddled face-down onto the concrete, moaning, gripping himself into a big wad of flesh, moaning still. At the door she looked briefly down at him, swung open the metal, hinges squealing, saying: "Got what it took, hey John Henry, you got it." Then she climbed up into the flat green cornfield.

Mildred Motley opened her eyes in time to see a dark green pickup truck pull off and park at the side of the road in front of her house. Inside was a light-haired man and in the bed of the truck was a yelping bear of a bird dog. It had a rope around its neck—needs a chain, Mildred Motley thought, a chain or a hunk of poison meat—and its mouth was a cage of bared teeth. The man jumped out of the truck, a package the size of a shoebox in his hands; he walked up the sidewalk where the waves of grass fell back and admitted passage. As he moved closer, Mildred Motley noticed that his eyes were like blue raspberries; she liked raspberries. It was three o'clock in the afternoon.

"Have a package for Miss Mildred Plonk," the man said, his eyes gaping raspberries. "You wouldn't happen to be Miss Mildred, would you?" He smiled a flicker of a smile and his dog started yelping, tugging at its rope, flailing around the bed of the pickup. "That's Ralph, my dog, he's crazy. Sometimes he don't even recognize me."

"I've seen a dog take a man's hand off in a matter of seconds," said Mildred Motley, blinking her eyes.

"Don't say," he said and set the package on top of the porch railing. Mildred Motley untucked her knees, put her feet side by side on the floor. The package clung like a tick to the wood of the porch railing. "I seen a dog eat a cat, fur and all."

"Have a way, dogs, don't they?"

"Sure do." The man was looking around the porch, around the yard, around her, but not exactly at her, and Mildred Motley found her hand straightening out a loose strand of hair. "Say listen, Miss Mildred, I could use a drink of something. You got something cold to drink? I been clear to Hamblen County to-day." He had a puckered scar down the side of one cheek that Mildred Motley was busy fixing in her mind, smoothing it out, destroying it.

"I said I could use a drink of something."

"A drink?" she said, startled, the scar inlaid in her mind, festering there. "Would you like a drink?"

"Yeh, I think I could use a drink of something." On her feet at once, Mildred Motley eased toward the screen door, hands tugging on her skirt folds, hands and mind straightening out wrinkles. Just then the dog broke free from its rope, like a bullet, Mildred Motley thought instantly, like a goddamn bullet, and dashed enraged and yelping toward her front porch. The man lunged for the screen door, opened it, pushed her inside, jumped inside himself, then let the door slam shut behind them. The dog, a mangle of teeth and fur and noise, knocked itself against the screen, slobbered on the mesh, barked and slobbered and knocked.

"Told you," he said. "Don't even know me half the time."

"You should kill it or something."

"Hell no, Ralph's a good hunting dog, he'll tire himself out in a while."

They stood in Mildred Motley's living room and watched Ralph beat his muzzle against the screen until finally he tucked his tail between his legs and lay down on the porch, yawning, drooling onto the wood. For a second Mildred Motley pictured the neighbor boy mowing Ralph down to the size of a single tooth, then she moved over to the couch that faced her coffee table.

"What about that drink?" the man said. He walked across the carpet, sat down on the couch, then crossed his legs, a triangular pocket of air opening up to the floor between them. "Name's Russell, by the way, Russell Ashmore from up to Morristown. Daddy was Clement Ashmore."

"I knew an Ashmore one time," Mildred Motley said and picked at the waistline of her skirt. "He got shot in Vietnam and sent back in a pine box though they said it wasn't much in it but a dog tag and some gold teeth."

"Don't say," Russell said, propping his hands behind his neck. Mildred Motley noticed that there were now three triangles in the lines of Russell's body. "He weren't no kin to me. What about that drink?"

"I have some frozen pink lemonade, take just a minute to make. You like lemonade?"

"Whatever you got is fine."

She crossed through the living room and into the kitchen, her right hand creeping up around her ears, flattening out a stray wisp of hair. Inside the freezer she took out a cylinder of lemonade, carried it over to the linoleum counter, then undid the plastic strip. Out in the living room Russell coughed and Mildred Motley began to smooth out the scar on his cheek again—the scar like a yellow snake in her brain, writhing when he moved his lips—began to iron out the skin of his cheek. She ran water in the sink, opening a cabinet while it ran, took out a mirror, careful to make no noise, and inspected her face. She put the mirror back in the cabinet. With one hand she dumped the frozen lemonade into a plastic pitcher and peered over the edge at the lemonade that lay whole on the bottom. Looks like pink shit, she thought, like pink shit on top of pink dog juice, then she let the pitcher fill up with water, and then she shut off the spigot. Stirring the water with a wooden spoon, she watched the pinkness spread until there was no water, only lemonade with white speckles that floated on the top. She filled two glasses and took them into the living room where Russell sat hunched over the coffee table, shuffling a deck of cards.

"You play cribbage?" he asked, shuffling. Mildred Motley set the glasses on the coffee table and took a seat in a straight-backed chair across from Russell.

"I know some tricks," she said and looked at him. Russell took a big swallow of lemonade, put the glass and the cards back on the table, then cocked his hands behind his neck again. Mildred Motley picked up the cards, making her jack appear on the bottom, then on the top, then in the middle of the deck, her fingers sinuating along the cards.

"I read cards myself," he said, "but that's pretty good," and he took the cards into his hands, shuffling them, putting four cards face up on the coffee table.

"That card there, that means you don't eat right, you know, don't eat regular." He pushed the card back at the deck; it slid inside and disappeared. "This queen here, it means you had a overbearing mother. See this scar?" He pointed at his cheek, twirling a finger above it.

"I see it," Mildred Motley said.

"My mother was a real bastard. Now this card means you probably don't like liver and that king means you probably would like Superman. Ever seen him?" Russell took another big swallow of lemonade with his eyes open so that they squinted onto the coffee table.

"No," said Mildred Motley.

"I seen him twice't, once for free. Know the ticket-taker. I could probably get you in for free."

"Don't say."

His eyes seemed to hang like ripe fruit in the middle of his face.

"The guy can fly and everything." Russell stood up from the couch, drained the lemonade—lips smacking, throat hopping—and walked to the screen door. At the door he turned around, saying "Pick you up at seven," then he was out on the porch, then the screen door slapped shut behind him. Mildred Motley got to her feet and followed him onto the porch, but he was walking toward the truck with the dog wagging violently beside him. As he crossed the street around the bed, he tapped the border lightly and the dog leapt up, like a cat, like a tiger, Mildred Motley thought, like a very big dog, and landed in the back of the pickup, his head and tail disembodied, wagging and wagging. Mildred Motley was trying to think of something to say, something important.

"Say, *you Russell*, what do you believe in?"

But Russell jumped into the driver's seat. Then he rolled down his window, shouting "Truth," starting the engine, shouting "Justice, Miss Mildred," jumping the truck into gear, "The American Way!" laughing with his mouth wide—red and white, teeth flashing, exposed and white—and then the pickup pulled out, dipped down a hill, smoke in a black tail behind him, through the tobacco fields until only a string of black smoke stuck up in the green distance. And then he was gone.

Mildred Motley picked up her package and took it into the house, into the bathroom. She sat on the toilet for a while, pulled herself together, then she opened the package; inside were her tennis shoes (new laces), three packs of Juicy Fruit chewing gum (unopened), and a smoky-glass bottle of paregoric. Reading the instructions briefly, she opened the bottle and swallowed three capfuls of smoky-colored liquid, recapped it, set it in the medicine cabinet. Finally she walked into her bedroom, letting her mind see a tractor trailer hit a speeding pickup truck, letting her mind destroy that picture, letting a vine of raspberries hang down right before her eyes, then she lay down on the bed to wait. To lay in wait for the medicine to take effect.

The Raising

Of the eight matrons perched like pigeons around two identical card tables, Mrs. Bertram Eastman was the lone childless woman. Her husband, in whom—she was sure—the fault lay, only confounded this burden she'd borne for thirty years, fixing a funny look on his face every time the subject came up and saying, in a voice soft as solemnity itself, "Spare the child and spare the rod, Mrs. Eastman." But he was like that, a nitwit, and half the time she never knew what he was talking about. Still, being a woman of industry, Mrs. Eastman took up the slack of impotence by becoming an expert on children and motherhood. She was renowned in the gin rummy set, in the Daughters of the Confederacy set, and perhaps in the whole area of East Tennessee, renowned and widely quoted for her running commentary on child-rearing.

"A child is like a new boot," she'd say and pause with the dramatic flair of a born talker. "You take that boot and wear it and at first it blisters your foot, pains you all over, but the time comes it fits like a glove and you got a dutiful child on your hands." What she had missed in experience, Mrs. Eastman overcame with pithy insight; what she lacked as human collateral in a world of procreation, Mrs. Eastman guaranteed with sheer volume. She was a specialist in armchair mothering.

_A steady hum of a general nature had settled over the women playing at both tables, punctuated by an occasional snap of a card, but like a foghorn in the midst of a desert the voice of Mrs. Eastman rose and fell in every ear. She was explaining, for the third time since seven o'clock, the circumstances that led to Little Darryl, the melungeon orphan boy, who would come to live at her house the very next morning. A child! In her own home! She couldn't get over it. Her brain worked at the idea with a violence akin to despair turning upside-down and her hair, from some internal cue, dropped onto her forehead a large, stiff curl that flopped from side to side as if to let off steam. Mrs. Eastman, although not fat, was a formidable personage, stout and big-boned and not unlike the bouncer in a hard-bitten country bar. Mr. Eastman was the tiniest man in Hawklen County. Just yesterday he had come home and told her, out of the blue, that he was bringing Little Darryl out from Eastern State and into their home—one two three and like a bolt of electricity she was a mother. She couldn't get over it.

Little Darryl was thirteen years old and of "origin unknown," a poor abandoned charity case dumped from orphanage to orphanage since the day his faceless mother—unfit and unwed, Mrs. Eastman knew for a certainty—dropped him off in the middle of the canned-goods section of the Surgoinsville A&P. He was discovered beside the creamed corn, eating an unhealthy peanut butter and jelly sandwich. The "origin unknown" part delighted Mrs. Eastman: Little Darryl would be *her* child, sprung as mysteriously and as certainly into her care as a baby of her own making. O, she would make a lawyer out of him, distill the taint of his blood like meltwater. She would recreate the boy in her own image and watch him tower among men in her old age.

"Smart as a *whip*, the social worker told Mr. Eastman," Mrs. Eastman said in a loud, confidential voice. At her table were old Mrs. Cowan, the Methodist preacher's wife; Mrs. Jenkins, the wife of the Jenkins Hardware Jenkinses; and Mrs. Talley, wife of Hubert Talley, the local butcher. Mrs. Eastman had given each one advice, off and on, for thirty years, from Mrs. Talley's redheaded boy who was thirty years old and no good, right down to Mrs. Jenkins' six-year-old who still sucked her thumb and was a "mistake."

"You said that ten minutes ago, Eloise," Mrs. Jenkins told Mrs. Eastman, "and you said he was a genius before that." Mrs. Jenkins was playing North to Mrs. Eastman's South. "You said he was a genius that wasn't understood and you ain't even met him yet."

"Made him a lawyer already, too," said Mrs. Talley, looking calmly over Mrs. Jenkins' shoulder, her lips screwed up in concentration.

"Ida Mae Talley!" cried Mrs. Jenkins. "Put you in the East and straightway you cheat left and right."

"For your general information," Mrs. Eastman said and tossed her curl, like a hook, back up into her beehive hairdo, "for your edification, Little Darryl scored in the 'excessively bright' range on three different tests."

"I am most certainly not cheating," said Mrs. Talley. "I seen those kings three minutes ago."

"God loves all the little children, smart and stupid, black and white," old Mrs. Cowan said with a smile so bright that her lips appeared to retreat back into her gums. She was the simple-minded member of the women's club although, somehow, her children had grown up to be wildly successful bankers and businessmen in the county, as if to intimate that children, even life, were too muddled a factor to control entirely. For this reason old Mrs. Cowan said nothing that was really heard, did nothing that was really seen, and existed in the main as a hand in gin rummy, or as a how-de-do on the Methodist Church steps every Sunday morning. She was incapable of taking sound advice, given in good faith, by even the best of friends. Deep in her bowels Mrs. Eastman believed her to be the most wicked woman of her acquaintance, the most deceitful as well as the most dangerous, and to hold, somewhere behind her idiocy, a hidden ace in the hole.

"God may be well and good on Sundays," Mrs. Eastman said, leveling her eyes like shotgun bores toward old Mrs. Cowan's western position. "But God Hisself don't have to raise no boy geniuses at a moment's notice. Pass me one of those green mints, Vivian." She stretched her free hand toward Mrs. Jenkins. "The white ones give me the morning sickness."

"They come in the same box, Eloise. Green and white. In the same damn box." Mrs. Jenkins, whose mints and home provided this evening's entertainment for the club, shut her cards with a click, laid them carefully facedown on the table, then folded her arms like hemp cord and stared at Mrs. Eastman. She looked ready to pounce in panther fashion across the table, to defend her territory with a beast's wit. Mrs. Eastman had on her patient expression, the one she recommended for children with colic.

"I only meant to point out that I *read* somewheres that they put more dye in the white mints than they do in the green, that's all. They start out gray and add twice't the dye to turn them white. Scientific fact. Twenty schoolchildren alone have died in Detroit, Michigan, from a pound of white mints. Now think about *that*."

"All I know," said Mrs. Jenkins, rising clumsily from her chair, "is we've had these same mints for fifteen years and I never heard a word till now. I'm going to put whip cream on my jello if you'll excuse me."

"I didn't read it till last week," Mrs. Eastman called over her shoulder, then she lowered her voice until only the whole room could hear: "Don't either of you tell a dead man, but she's on par*tic*ular edge tonight strictly because her boy was found pig drunk, with a hair ribbon in his mouth, underneath the 11-E overpass. No clothes on him anywhere."

"O," said old Mrs. Cowan. "He was the finest acolyte our church ever had."

"No more he ain't," Mrs. Eastman said happily. "Comes of no discipline."

"Now, now," Mrs. Talley said, watching herself thumb through Mrs. Jenkins' cards, "You ain't exactly the one, Eloise"—here she paused to exchange one of her cards with one in the other pile—"you ain't exactly the one to pass judgment on a drunk, now are you?"

"Well, Mrs. Ida *Mae* Talley." Mrs. Eastman sneered on the "Mae." "Are you sinuating that my husband is a drunk?"

"That's for you to know, Eloise," she said, "and me to hear over coffee."

The truth of the matter was that, although Mr. Eastman sat in his law office with the door shut to clients and associates alike and drank corn whiskey from a Dixie cup, reading obscure poetry and even more obscure philosophy from dusty, dead-looking bindings, he was not a drunk. He was merely partial to alcohol, had told Mrs. Eastman more than once that he and whiskey were blood-related, on better terms with one another than anyone living or dead he'd ever known. Mrs. Eastman believed him through a rare faculty of reflexive apathy, a sixth sense she applied to all situations beyond her ken and control. Once, when Mr. Eastman brought home a litter of eight mongrel dogs, payment for services rendered from one of his poverty clients (who were the only ones he seemed to have, crowded into his office anteroom with chickens and moonshine and quart jars full of pennies clutched under their arms, the room always a three-ring circus to the point that each newly hired legal secretary had but to walk in the door before she quit and walked back out), Mrs. Eastman, in a reflex as immediate as a sneeze, stepped on the dogs' tails, ate the dogs' fur in her potatoes and greens, got nipped on the calves in the middle of dogfights, and she never knew the difference. The dogs existed only as the vaguest of doubts in her mind, much as the person and behavior of Mr. Eastman, and eventually, one by one, the dogs skulked emphatically from the premises and trotted off westward, as if in search of something that either would caress them passionately or kick them viciously. Leave bad enough alone, Mrs. Eastman always said, as well as, Never look a gifted horse in the mouth.

"Leave bad enough alone *I* always say," Mrs. Eastman told Mrs. Talley. "If I had a boy thirty year old and still at home, I wouldn't make no sinuations on nobody else."

"The best, O! O!" said old Mrs. Cowan, almost luringly. "The best acolyte we ever had."

Both women stared at her.

"Attention ladies!" Mrs. Jenkins called from the kitchen door. She held a tray of eight green jello molds, each topped with pear-shaped smidgens of whipped cream. "Laura June here wants to say goodnight," she said. "Say goodnight, Laura June." Laura June, who was under the tray in her mother's hands, just stood and looked stupidly at the seven crooked smiles fastened maternally on the faces of the women's club. Under her arm showed the hind legs and tail of a tabby cat, and she wore a pink nightgown, hiked up at the waist from the furious squirms of the cat. Because her thumb was plunged up to the knuckle into her mouth, Laura June had difficulty saying goodnight, so she just stood and stared, stupidly, at all the smiles.

"That there is what I call a real teddy bear," Mrs. Talley said sweetly. "What's that there teddy bear's name, honey?"

Laura June turned her head in the direction of Mrs. Talley, squinting her eyes, and the cat, as though synchronized puppet-like to her movements, turned its head around and squinted at the women with two uneven green eyes that matched the color of the jello. One of its eyes had an ugly yellow pustule on the rim, making the whole eye look like an open wound in the act of rankling. Laura June unplugged her mouth long enough to say "Name's Darryl Lee Roy," then she quickly plugged the thumb back, as if any second something more important might fall out into the open.

"Why isn't that just the cutest thing!" Mrs. Eastman cried and clapped her hands in the air over the card table. "Come over here, honey, Mama Eastman has a secret for you." Laura June stayed put; the cat blinked its eyes and only one of them opened again. It appeared to be winking suggestively at Mrs. Eastman. "I have a little boy coming to my house that has the very same name," she said. "Little Darryl."

"Time for Laura June to go to bed," said Mrs. Jenkins. "Go to bed, Laura June." Laura June turned obediently toward a door across the room and stalked stiff-legged across the wooden slats with the cat's head bouncing behind her like a gibbous growth. At the door she stopped, facing the room, and caught Mrs. Eastman's eye. There was an expression of malignancy on her face. She dropped the thumb and the hand wandered with a will of its own to the side of her face where it started to scratch a cheek. It might have been a large, pink spider dropped incredibly there to spin a cobweb.

"It's a lie!" she shouted abruptly and the cat meowed and then both were gone into the dark recesses of the house.

II

The mountains spliced at the southernmost tip of the city limits, then diverged northward to form the east and west boundaries of Hawklenville where Mr. Bertram Eastman lived. An ambitious person could climb to the top of that southern splice—named Devil's Nose by the first Methodist settlers—could sit on one of the numerous granite slabs found there, and he would notice that the town appears to be a discolored blemish in the middle of a dark green arrowhead. If that person were ambitious indeed, he would climb a tree and see the land beyond the mountains, land welling out for miles, green with tobacco, brown with freshly tilled soil, and still farther, the cusp of something huge and dusky-blue. But he would see no people. Though these mountains were the town's sole measure of eminent height, a stranger well-versed in the world would point out that they were only foothills, mere knurls in the great body of the Appalachians. Still, from their summits, one could see no people. They are *that* high, Mr. Eastman often said, but quietly and mostly to himself, they are high enough.

From his small back porch, or from what might have been a porch had he chosen to call it one, preferring the word *veranda* because it "sounded like a sigh," Mr. Eastman was watching the last tendrils of light skid away over the top of the moutains. Mr. Eastman, a man not balding but bald, sat in a plastic lawn chair and sipped corn whiskey from a Dixie cup. His shoulders cocked slightly forward and his head tilted slightly backward, giving him the appearance (as the more flexible gossips of the town were quick to mimic) of neither coming nor going. At the moment, though, he was poised over a precipice, at the edge of something, and somehow the boy, Little Darryl, was the nub to which his mind clung. Tomorrow he would come and tomorrow something—he didn't know what—something would happen, for tomorrow Little Darryl would come.

Beads of sweat, tiny as dewdrops, eased from the crown of his head and slid unhindered down the back of his neck. So quickly did they fall, and so brazenly, they could have been the tears of a brokenhearted old woman too tired for pretense. Night had fallen and the mountains crouched against the sky, darker even than the night.

Experience had taught Mr. Eastman that the mountains themselves were deceptive, mute purveyors of nothing but bulk. To the tourist, as he had been when he first brought his wife to the town, they were beautiful, rumpled across the horizon like an immense and living snake. He recalled an incident from those earlier days. They had been walking down Main Street, he and his newly-wed wife, he arm in arm with a woman who was so

striking and so lovely, all the more so because of her height and
his lack of it, that he thought he might be crushed under the
weight of his own pride. They had walked in silence for many
minutes, nodding sociably at the passersby, when he noticed the
mountains around them, as though for the first time.

"They are like a great undulating serpent, Eloise," he told her,
and he was trying to profess his love for her and for their new
home. Her eyes almost the color of ripe raspberries, she looked
first at the moutains, then down at him, and she stared into his
face with an expression that may have been utter tenderness. At
last she fluttered her eyelashes and, looking vaguely toward the
mountains, said: "Do tell." The mountains were no longer beautiful to Mr. Eastman, hadn't been perhaps from the incident on;
and neither was his wife. No longer did he see the mountains
surge upward as living things, no longer was the town, nor the
county of Hawklen, a place where north and south and west and
east converged into only one thing: the place to be. He had been
deceived.

This boy, this Little Darryl, would be his salvation.

"Yoo-hoo!" came his wife's voice through the entranceway,
through the hallway, through the kitchen and onto the back veranda where he started, like a frightened sparrow, in the lawn
chair. "I'm home!"

Mr. Eastman bent down and set his Dixie cup on the floor,
then he placed his hands, one grottoed in the bowl of the other,
into his lap. Patiently, keenly, like a man for whom time was as
yet unborn, he waited to be found out by his wife. An excess of
amplified noise, her greeting was meant for the house and not
for him, but in a short time she would work her way through
every room until she found him out. She was tenacious in that
way, could find anything lost, stolen, or converted, except the
truth. She had a gift of activity at its most inessential where-
abouts, a kind of feverish sprinting in place that left her wrung-
out and triumphant and as blind as a newt. Mr. Eastman believed he was safe from her, his wife of thirty years, because,
when you got right down to it, she didn't know shit from apple
butter; and without distinctions the rage to live was merely a
delirious murmur. Despite the sounds of a bull ox, Mrs. Eastman, he felt, was a murmurer.

"*There* you are," Mrs. Eastman said and poked her head between the screen door and the door frame. It hung there in space like a giant full moon whose face had a coarse, sketchy expression. The least cloud would obscure any resemblance to humanity it may have had. Or so it seemed to Mr. Eastman who sat quietly with his hands in his lap.

"Here I am," Mr. Eastman said.

Here and there across the back yard a group of crickets screeched to one another in duets, in off-beat duets, in those insistent and eerie cries of utterly invisible creatures involved in communication. *Cheezit!* they said. *Cheezit!*

"Listen to those bugs," Mrs. Eastman said and stepped onto the veranda. She let the screen door slam shut behind her, its springs squealing, and the crickets paused for a measure, then started back up again. With her hands fastened securely onto her hips, elbows akimbo, she peered out into the back yard in order to pin down the source of the sound coming from everywhere and nowhere. "I declare they sound like they're in painful love. Bugs do fall in love and set up house together just like anybody. It's nature is what it is." Mr. Eastman said nothing and sat tight, as if he were just hanging in a closet without any insides; he wanted to pat his wife kindly on the cheek or else smack her very hard in the middle of her face. But he did nothing at all, could have been dead except for the heart pounding madly between the places he breathed.

"Buddy Ruth Quarles run off this morning with that retarded taxicab driver. Took almost everything they owned. In case you're interested." She slapped and killed a periwinkle green insect, then continued on in a cheerful tone. A dollop of hair ticked coquettishly onto her forehead. "Took the TV, took the radio, took the silverware. Took the sofa and the phonograph. Took ever light bulb in the house. Didn't take that half-grown boy of hers. Last anybody saw of Mr. Quarles, he took off down 11-E with a butcher knife, wearing a pair of socks and green pants. He had to borrow the butcher knife. Mr. Eastman, are you listening to me?"

"No, Mrs. Eastman," he said. "I am not."

"Ida Mae said she hadn't known the taxicab driver but three weeks, and him so simple to begin with. They did it with a U-Haul hitched to the taxicab."

"Mrs. Eastman," said Mr. Eastman.

"Can't figure out, though, what she *sees* in him. He had that wart in the corner of his eye. Puckered and bobbed ever time he opened his mouth. I can't figure it. And him so simple too."

Mr. Eastman reached for his Dixie cup, squinting out into the night settled over his yard. It appeared to him to be the inside of a huge windowless box set on its side out in the middle of nowhere. The stars, pricking out relentlessly, didn't fit into his picture.

"I foretold it long ago. Time and again I said, If he don't kill her first, he won't never know where she'll be or what's she's doing there. I foretold it twice in the past two years. If she's not six feet under, I said, no telling where she is. There you have it."

"Perhaps she's happy, Mrs. Eastman."

"Well *I like that!*" Mrs. Eastman cried and stomped three paces to the edge of the veranda, then stomped the three paces back. She was furious, looking at him as she might at some bear who still hibernated in the chafe of summer, and her hair bristled like burs along the top of her head. "Happy, Mr. Eastman, is what those bugs have. Any *nor*mal human being might know that already. Any *nor*mal human being might know that happy is a word the government made up. What will our son think? I'll tell you what he'll think, he'll think his daddy's shoes are too little to grow into, that's what. You'll be a stigmatism to him all the days of his life!"

Again, Mr. Eastman sat tight. Thought and action in his wife, usually by tongue but sometimes otherwise, were almost simultaneous in her, rather like thunder and lightning, and Mr. Eastman was forever surprised by the coincidence. For him there was by necessity a gap between the two, first deep thought and much later decisive action. And it was true: it had taken him thirty years to secure a son.

"Do you hear me, Bertram Eastman?" she asked. Stomping up and back, her hair at loose ends, her shadow stomping crabbed and backwards behind her through the light from the house, she made Mr. Eastman want to shout; want to scream out madly; made him want to take the box of his back yard and the night and his wife and fling the whole of them over that impenetrable black scar of the mountains. Instead he said absolutely nothing and, too, the silence within him grew absolute.

"Do you *hear* me?"

"I hear you very well, Mrs. Eastman."

"Our son is a responsibility. He's a responsibility for bad and for worse, for sickness and disease, forever and forever, till the dead do us part. He's responsibility is what this boy's made of."

"I know what little boys are made of," he said, raising himself to leave. So soaked with sweat was the back of his collar that it crept toward his collarbone and felt like a cold hand at his throat. Out in the yard the crickets seemed to have gone mad in the intcrim of their conversation. *Cheezit! cheezit! cheezit!* they sang. Cheee-*zit!* If his wife said anything, he couldn't hear her for the crickets.

III

Little Darryl's people, the melungeons, came from Goins Hollow, a cul-de-sac at the base of Devil's Nose from whence there was only one exit: a deep green bottleneck steeped in poison ivy and ridden with underbrush and so utterly hidden that the inhabitants themselves were known to leave and never return, set suddenly adrift in the outside world. Brown-eyed and maize-colored, thcy wedlocked themselves, cheated on themselves, co-alesced with abandon, and produced either geniuses or idiots. They had no in-betweens. They loved each other or they killed each other, and still they endured in Goins Hollow; their endur-ance preccded the first Methodist settlers by many hand-counted years. On a vivid autumn day the smoke of their fires, beckoning upward like unformed fingers, was clearly visible from the town of Hawklenville, but not one soul in Hawklenville ever looked at it.

The melungeon blood, although not their expcrience, was fe-cund as a loam in the body of Little Darryl, the orphan, and by the age of five he knew the appetites of a very old man. He knew when to lie outright and when to tell a lie honestly, when to cheat and when to win fairly. He knew when to be given and when to steal someone blind. He even knew when to attack a problem face-forward, and when to beat a noble retreat into the next county. He was thirteen years old, of a conspicuous unknown origin, and he had lived in nine separate orphanages, one of which burned down mysteriously.

"They got the papers that's stuck to me," Little Darryl told the orphan boys who sat roosting on the next cot, "and there ain't nothing but for me to go with them. They got the papers."

"You could burn them papers," suggested the littlest boy, writhing himself in embarrassment so that the row of boys tilted sideways like a wave washing through. Each little boy had a scar of some kind on some part of his body, and each boy loved Little Darryl with a passion that drew blood. He had seen to that.

"You would, would you," said Little Darryl and leaned over and flipped the littlest boy's nose until he bellowed out. "They got the machines that can resurrect a million a me. You burn one paper and they make ten more. You burn ten papers and they fill a library with them. You burn down a library and they fill the whole shittin world with paper. They got you up one side and down the other."

"You could run away from here," a boy with a cauliflower ear said, "could run to Kingdom Come from here."

The littlest boy sniffed and said: "That's what I meant back then."

"I already done that once't," Little Darryl said. "They come at me with three cop cars and six guns. They had the papers that's stuck to me. The highest mountain and the lowest hole, they got you if they got them papers that they think is you."

"*I* don't have no papers on *me*," said the boy with a cauliflower ear. He let out a yell and thumped his chest to prove himself. All the little boys fell to scuffling, then they cheered and the cot skittered a few inches along the floor.

"It's because you ain't never done nothing worth the proving of it," Little Darryl said and smacked the boy on his cauliflower ear. They all settled down after that.

"These here people I ain't never seen nor seen their house might think they know what my paper says, but they don't know me. I reckon I got the upper hand under them, I reckon I know who I am." Little Darryl puffed himself up with air, standing slack-kneed on the bed with his shoes on. "I seen worse predicaments." The little boys stared up at him with the expressions of crows strung on a telephone wire. They flapped their arms and stared. "I seen the worser and the worst and they's nothing I seen that could make me forget myself in it. Pain's nothing to the forgetting yourself from it. I know who I am."

"Darryl!" cried the social worker. "Get your shoes off that bed and on the floor." She had on a pink polyester pantsuit that clung to her legs and gave the appearance of a second skin shedding off from the waist down.

"Boooo," said all the little boys, punching each other.

"It's my bed," Little Darryl said. "I'll stand on my own bed with anything on."

"You go home today and you know it. Effective at seven o'clock A.M. it wasn't your bed any more."

"I'll stand on anybody's bed with anything on."

"Let's go," the social worker said grimly. With her free arm cocked in a triangle just above her waist, she held open the door and looked as if the least movement would make her pants disappear. The little boys waited expectantly, booing softly.

"I seen worse than you look on Monday morning," said Little Darryl and got down off the bed. The little boys cheered, scuffled, grew into a wad of arms and legs on top of the cot. At the door Little Darryl looked back into the dormitory room, then he spat viciously on the floor.

"I seen even worser," he said, but the little boys, scuffling, didn't look up again.

IV

"Excessively bright! Excessively bright!" Mrs. Eastman sang aloud, scattering motes of dust helter-skelter with her mud-colored featherduster. The dust settled down again just inches ahead of Mrs. Eastman's movement across the table. "O my boy, O yes *my* boy, O he is ex—*press*—ive—ly—bright!"

Up at cock's crow that morning (the cock one of Mr. Eastman's poverty payments), Mrs. Eastman rampaged through the dawn inside her house with a vengeance and a joy. She had attacked her floors and her ceilings, her walls, her knickknacks. She'd made, then unmade, then made again her beds. She did the same with Little Darryl. First he was a lawyer, then he was a president, then he was a brain surgeon. Nothing suited. She couldn't get over it, she was electrified. And when the doorbell rang she thought she'd liked to have had a heart murmur. With the hand that held the duster pressed against her chest, she prayed to God and sneezed violently. Dust floated everywhere like tiny messengers. A feeling came to her, at the base of her spine, and it said, Practice makes perfect! Pretty is as pretty does! These were the exact sentiments she had expressed, intuitively, to the women's club off and on for thirty years: real mothering would be her forte. She sneezed once more and felt powerful.

By the second ring from the doorbell Mrs. Eastman was prepared, so much so that when she opened the door she had on her wisdom expression, the one she recommended for children with homesickness. On her porch stood a pair of pink polyester pants and Little Darryl, who wore an oversized Prince Edward coat, collar turned up, and a brown fedora hat, brim turned down. His eyes peeped out from under his hat as though from inside a tank turret. Mrs. Eastman said the first thing to come to her mind.

"I didn't know he was such a colored child," she said and smiled maternally. The eyes inside the hat seemed to look through Mrs. Eastman and onto the entranceway carpet. "I could've mistook you for a pickaninny, little boy," she said sweetly.

"They's two people said that to me before and lived," said Little Darryl.

"I'll be running right along," the social worker told Mrs. Eastman, "if you'll just sign these documents. I already stopped by your husband's office."

"Looked more like one of them goddamn saloons to me," Little Darryl snarled, spitting through his teeth at a fly on the porch. "Smell't of it, too."

"We don't curse in this home, Darryl. We are gentlemen and ladies in this home. Gentlemen and ladies don't curse or spit."

He looked at her, his eyes slightly askew.

"Sign here," said the social worker, and Mrs. Eastman did.

"You might think that's me right there," Little Darryl said through his teeth. Mrs. Eastman could have sworn it came from the paper itself. "But I know where I stand."

"Why of course you do!" Mrs. Eastman cried. "You're on the

doorstep of your very own home!" She gave Little Darryl a hug, agitated by the goodness welling inside her like a carbonation, and he stood stiffly as a hanged man.

"From now on you touch me by permission," he said out of a corner of his mouth.

When they looked up the social worker was long gone.

"Food," said Mrs. Eastman. "You must be hungry, little boys are always hungry. They are hungry until they reach the age of twenty and then they are modern afterwards."

"I've eat but I could do it again if it was a roast beef with string beans."

Without another word Mrs. Eastman clucked and herded Little Darryl into the kitchen of her house. On his way he picked up two china cats, pilfering them into the pocket of his Prince Albert. A look of sublime pleasure, which Mrs. Eastman mistook for good adjustment, showed above the coat collar. He sidled up to a kitchen window, gazed sullenly onto the back yard with a hooded pucker around his eyes.

"Gentlemen don't wear hats on in their homes," said Mrs. Eastman. Her hands gripped and sliced on the roast as if performing an emergency operation on a still-live body.

"Lady," said Little Darryl, his eyes directed toward the back yard. "I don't like you. I don't like your house, I don't like your husband that I ain't even met. The onliest thing to keep me from the murder of you is if'n you pretend you don't see hear smell feel nor taste me. Do you understand me in that head a hair?"

"But I'm your mother." Mrs. Eastman paused, an expression of some awful recognition shrouding her nose and eyes and mouth. "Pretty is as pretty does," she said.

"You're nuts," he said, "and my mother was a thought my daddy thought for about three seconds. Serve me that roast beef with ketchup on it." He sat down at the table, pulling out a jackknife; the silver spoon and knife already on a place mat, he put in his pocket. He left the fork where it was.

"God loves all the little children," Mrs. Eastman said and her voice sounded very far away. "Black and white, smart and stupid."

"Serve it with ketchup and some mayo on the side, lady." In a rapid, choppy movement Little Darryl flipped open the jackknife and let the blade hang, for an instant, in the air like an unkept promise. "That God of yourn loves because they got the papers on Him a million years ago. You don't a bit more know who He is than you think you know who I am. I know worser."

"You!" screeched Mrs. Eastman. "You're a mistake!" Her hair and nerves were all unstrung. "I'm not your mother, you won't be a lawyer, you won't be." She couldn't think, and immediately, in a reflexive action, she shifted gears into the vaguest of doubts. Outside the rooster crooned an offbeat love song. "I'm going to call my husband," said Mrs. Eastman, dispassionately.

"Serve me the roast beef first," Little Darryl said, and Mrs. Eastman did, filling a plate with greasy slices that hunkered on top of each other in an orgy of flesh. "I ain't afraid of nobody that'd marry you."

While Mrs. Eastman was gone Little Darryl ate the roast beef and when he finished he roamed around, pocketing certain valuables. Inside the refrigerator he found a hamhock. He put it inside the coat, down near the waistline. Inside a drawer he found the silverware, and he put it all, including a soup ladle, into the front left pocket of the Prince Albert. It bulged outward like a cancerous tumor. He put the remains of the roast beef and a bottle of ketchup into the front right pocket. By the time Mrs. Eastman got back, there was very little left in her kitchen.

"He's on his way home," Mrs. Eastman told him, as if the matter were settled at last.

"Whoopee," said Little Darryl. He clinked when he spoke. "You're going to have to go upstairs." Briefly, but certainly, he flashed the jackknife in front of Mrs. Eastman. It caused her to remember a story she'd heard quite a time ago. "You're going to have to show me where your jewry is up there. I'll take my chances with them papers this time."

"You're just a little boy," Mrs. Eastman said. "Just a little children."

"They's bigger than me that's less. Upstairs, lady."

Mrs. Eastman breathed heavily up the stairs, and she felt her heart make little leaps, as though it might creep onto her tongue and expose something. Each crack in the wood of the floor struck her as the place to be, each piece of dust looked like the safest of sizes, and she studied them with the vigilance of a scientist. In the bedroom she had a horrible thought.

"You wouldn't hurt a lady would you?" she asked, but Little Darryl was already rooting through her dressing table. "You wouldn't hurt a lady *would you?*" she asked, a little louder. She got up on her bed and held tightly as a tick to the wood of the headboard. "*Would you?*"

Little Darryl turned around, his hands full of rings and bracelets and necklaces that dangled like liquids through his fingers. Along the lines of his face there slithered a configuration of sheer hatred.

"Lady," he said, almost tenderly, "I wouldn't touch a hair a your head for anything anywhere," and then he disappeared out of the bedroom.

"Rape!" Mrs. Eastman cried, but her heart wasn't in it.

When Mr. Eastman came home all he could hear were his wife's screams, and all he could see was a brown figure in the distance, the plumes of a rooster sticking out like an exhaust under its arms, and all he could think would be forever silent.

The Snipe Hunters

On a map the state of Tennessee is a rough parallelogram. At a glance, though, you can tell that the east and west sides are neither parallel nor equal. For instance, when I was a little girl, a governor by the name of Dunne changed all the interstate highway signs to read "Welcome to the Three States of Tennessee." He meant to point out to tourists the fact that not only were they crossing into a different state, but they were also in one of three separate places: East Tennessee, Middle Tennessee, or West Tennessee. In a strong sense this is true. However, in 1976 another governor changed the signs to read "Welcome to the Great State of Tennessee," and now tourists glide on through our state and are not privy to its secret.

My people are East Tennesseans, have been since James Patrick McGuire took a wild hair in 1783 and moved from Fermanagh County, Ireland, to White Pine in Jefferson County, Tennessee. According to the family rumor, he was a short and ugly one-legged man with a short, ugly temper, given to spurts of *dementia praecox* and, at times, to beating his wife. Otherwise, he is an unknown factor. But there we were, blossoming into Ashmores and Dinwiddies and Hitchings at each successive decade, branching from a one-legged man throughout the heart of East Tennessee.

Few of us ever leave home, or ever want to, save for those men who fight our country's battles overseas and who become lieutenants or heroes, or else become dead. We like it here; we like it fine, thank you. In fact, my Grandfather Ashmore, a very wise man in his way, once pointed out that if you took the state on its easternmost edge and lifted it, like a rug so to speak, everything and everyone in Middle and West Tennessee would go tumbling off into the Mississippi, but East Tennesseans would be caught by the mountains, would just burrow deeper into the hills. Of course, it would greatly facilitate our state's commerce, which is known for its cotton and other goods, to have everything bleed out naturally and quickly onto the Mississippi where large, empty boats are always waiting.

My grandfather has many such good ideas. When he really gets going they tumble from his mouth like watermelon seed. Sometimes they even clog up, due to a faulty gum plate that slips onto his tongue along with two front teeth. He is an eighty-nine-year-old man with none of his faculties impaired, unless, of course, teeth are a faculty. Just on general principles, I believe he will never die.

The thing is, I go to see him today. This morning Timothy came around my office with a note from Grandfather inviting me over for supper. He is an odd one, this Timothy, partially because he blew half his head off in a Russian roulette game twenty years ago, and therefore scattered most of his wits into random pockets throughout his brain. But every once in a while a circuit will connect and then Timothy will have the uncanny sense of a terrestrial demon. For example, this morning he hung around my desk after giving me Grandfather's note, just to make sure no money would change hands. I send my grandfather fifty dollars every week like clockwork, a fact of which Timothy is vaguely aware and is driven to investigate. Sometimes I give him five dollars and he says, "Direc'ly," meaning he'll take it straight to Grandfather, then he goes and buys soda pop and picture postcards. He is a collector of sorts, and the walls of his room in Grandfather's house are covered with ten-cent scenic views.

"Thank you, Timothy," I say, when he hands me the note. His black head has a bell-shaped aspect since pieces of it have been forfeited by bullet, and he holds his chin in the loose support of one black hand.

"Mmm," he says and shuffles forward until his thighs rest against the desktop. "Mmm."

"*Thank* you." He nods and grins and stands there, cupping his chin with a quizzical-keen expression. At times I believe he is more sane than anyone I have ever met. For a fact, my grandfather enjoys his company.

"You better get back to the house, Timothy, it's almost lunchtime." He nods seriously, suddenly aware that his mission is accomplished and he must leave empty-handed. Instantly he assumes his dead expression, vacant eyes and slack mouth, an expression that effectively wards off all outside communication.

"Night," he says, meaning "goodbye," and away he shuffles, chin in hand.

I look at Grandfather's note again. It can mean only one thing: he has broken a code of some sort. This is a game we have played for years, twenty to be exact, and we are quite serious about it—dead serious, in fact. My grandfather and I are snipe hunters.

I experienced my first snipe hunt when I was eight years old, and after I told Grandfather about it we developed the game. This is what happened. Some friends of mine from the grade school invited me on a hayride through Dumplin Valley, located in the northeast corner of Jefferson County. A little past sunset they came by and picked me up and off we went in the bed of the haywagon. They were giggling and whispering and shutting flashlights on and off at the dirt road that oozed by ever so slowly behind the wagon. Something was up. When we got to Dumplin Valley, a place out in the middle of nowhere with stiff pine forests that jut out like fangs into the sky, when we got there, the wagon pulled off at the side of the road and stopped. Everyone clambered out. Except for the flicker of flashlights, the night was as thick and dark as bear's fur. Over by the wagon cab, Ernest, somebody's big brother, lit a cigarette and his face shown pale and bored. The company of eight-year-olds was probably beneath his dignity.

"We're going to hunt snipes, Elizabeth!" someone shouted and everyone cheered. There was an excitement in the air, an excitement akin to the smell of roasted meat right before dinner. With the flashlights bobbing and weaving, we set off in a pack into the forest. We walked and walked and occasionally somebody would yell, "I see one!" Then the excitement would mount. I couldn't see a thing, but, of course, I didn't have a flashlight. At last someone found a hole in the middle of a mat of pine needles.

Everyone grew almost hysterical over this hole; that was a snipe hole, they said. It was agreed that I would stand guard over the hole while they looked for more holes. So I sat down on the needles and stared, armed with a big stick to beat to death anything that stuck its head out. I stared and stared.

For a few minutes I could make out the glimmer of flashlights and the snap of twigs, but after a while—nothing. It was awfully lonely, the loneliest I've every been. No moon was out, no stars, no east or west, only this small black hole in the ground out in the middle of nowhere. I was profoundly lost, lost to death, Grandfather would say, meaning "utterly." I grew very familiar with the hole; it seemed to center the strangeness of the entire forest.

Suffice to say, by daybreak I found my way home, hitched a ride into Jefferson City on a tractor. Later I discovered from Grandfather that snipes, a kind of woodcock, have not existed in East Tennessee since the days of the primordial swamp lizards. Then we developed the game. The point of our snipe hunt is the hunt itself. Though snipes do not exist, still you must hunt, you must hunt and hunt or else you are utterly lost, lost to death, without the familiarity of even a small black hole.

So we, Grandfather and I, that is, are always on the lookout for codes, hints, and messages to facilitate the hunt. For instance, just the other day I found an interesting article in the *Jefferson Standard,* our local newspaper which, by the way, has won many state awards for its Republican editorials. Such a newspaper is full of useful hints. This article said: "Due to the frequency of his hoarse and inarticulate elephant cries, the original movie Tarzan has been moved from his double-occupancy room to a private suite in the Oakdale Nursing Home." The point, of course, is not just *what* was said, which may or may not be misleading, but *how* it was said, which is rarely misleading. This, then, is the nature of an undecoded hint. My grandfather loves this particular hint.

I place Grandfather's note in the upper right hand drawer of my desk, filing it carefully under "A." As secretary for a prominent law firm in town—Hale and Hale Associates—I pride myself on the efficient disposal of all information. Both Mr. Hap and Mr. Hap, Jr., as well as several other professional people, have spoken highly of my efficiency. The two years I spent at a prestigious state university left me fairly well-educated and certainly more efficient. In fact, I was once engaged to a fraternity boy there. During the course of an activity known as "rush," however, three of his friends pushed him out a window on the fourth floor of their fraternity house, and his neck snapped like a twig on the pavement below. It was an accident; they were drunk and having a good time. I left the university and went home soon thereafter.

It is a quarter to five. In a few minutes Mr. Hap, Jr. will come into my office and shoot the breeze until five o'clock, then we can all go home. On my desk all papers and folders are neatly aligned at the edges, all pens and pencils tucked away in their respective drawers. The dust cover is snug over the typewriter to my right, warding off the grit that is deadly to a well-oiled machine. I take great pleasure in following the factory instructions to the letter, and consequently this IBM is practically factory-fresh. Other secretaries I know, who will remain unnamed, are inattentive with their machines and therefore constantly wrestle with a hiccupping return button here or a stubborn tab-set there, wasting precious minutes.

Mr. Hap, Jr.'s head suddenly bobs just inside my office door. Suspended in the air, his head reminds me of those carnival kewpie dolls—gleaming bald head, pudgy cheeks, a pinkish smile that won't come unstuck no matter what the wear and tear. He is quite a character, never misses a trick. It is common knowledge that his father forced him into the law practice, but because of his flexible nature, he has made a good show of it. Unfortunately, he shows no knack for making money, a bone of contention between him and his father.

"Ding-dong," he says and the pink lips part slightly. "The world ends in six and a half minutes." He is in his silly-serious mood, smiling and smiling, entering the office with his arms flung over his head like a grown Chicken Little. As if to assess the state of affairs, his eyes dart back and forth across the top of my desk until, apparently satisfied, he edges closer and swings a hip onto the lip of the typewriter stand. Though half-sitting, he appears to be in perpetual motion. He never misses a trick and everything is a trick not to be missed. For the life of me, after every conversation with Mr. Hap, Jr., I can never remember a word that was said.

"What a day," he says, expelling some air, juggling his vision between me, the desktop, and the window to our left. I wait for something more to go on.

"That Devotie case is going to blow up any day now. Judge Hanson's fit to be tied and me running my legs off between the courthouse and city hall. I tell you what, it's been a real day." He sucks in some breath that whistles hollowly inside his cheek; his eyes rove the room and come to rest on his wristwatch. In a flash his body is back in motion, standing upright, moving off toward the door.

"Let's go home," he says and is gone.

The smell of his after-shave lingers in the office, then succumbs to the more pervasive scent of metal and ink. In seconds there is no trace whatsoever left of Mr. Hap, Jr. Grandfather would say that he is one of the lost people, hasn't a clue and doesn't even know it. I pick up my handbag, cross through the office, through the anteroom and on outside the office building. Mr. Hap will lock up later this evening, after the sessions court closes. Interestingly enough, all thefts in Jefferson County occur after a lock has been forced; an unlocked door in this county is as good as four large policemen armed to the teeth. As my grandfather says, there is always the taint of an unknown behind unlocked doors, while a locked door merely presents a duty in the course of a criminal job description.

O, but it is a fine day, a snipe hunt kind of day. Great pregnant-looking clouds are swelled to bursting over the southwest horizon, and the sharp point of a flock of geese pricks the outermost cloud, disappears inside, heading farther south. The streets are full now with people off work and going home. I know most everyone and receive businesslike nods from the men, flickering smiles from the women. But I am busily hunting among them. The danger is that, by becoming too familiar with one's surroundings, things recede into invisibility—they do not exist and, by extension, neither do you. So I keep a sharp lookout, not a moment's lapse of attention for me, thank you.

To get to Grandfather's house I need only walk down Main Street, then take a right onto Dogwood. All the storefronts on

Main boast bulky-knit sweaters and heavy galoshes, anticipating winter by two months; it is all a person can do to hold tight with the present. I notice Miss Ruby Lee Prigmore eyeing the winter lingerie in the Belk department store window, sizing up, testing seams with her discriminating shopper's glance. All small towns have their local gossips, and Miss Ruby is ours. She has known my family since the days of Grandfather's youth, and occasionally she corners me to pump for more up-to-date information. However, at the moment she is engrossed in lingerie, but—no— she shifts her field of vision in my direction, her radar as keen as any bat's.

"Elizabeth, dear," she says, eyes sizing me up though her mind has shifted gears from lingerie to information.

"I was just telling Sarah the other day, I said, 'Sarah, it's been ages since I saw that Elizabeth Ashmore, and I wonder what she's up to.' I said those very words. And here you are, big as life."

"Yes'm."

"And where are you off to, young lady, some gentleman no doubt, some dark, handsome stranger?"

Miss Ruby would like to see me get married although she and her sister remain unmarried with a vengeance. A story floats around town that Miss Ruby was once engaged to a man from Knoxville, a Fuller brush man, who during the course of an intimate dinner asked Miss Ruby whether or not her eyelashes were fake or real. Affronted, Miss Ruby said, "Pull one of the damn things and see," and the man was never seen in town again. Possibly he changed his sales route. Nevertheless, Miss Ruby and Miss Sarah love a big wedding and are present at all but spur-of-the-moment elopements.

"No'm, I'm going to supper at Grandfather's."

"O yes, fine man your grandfather, a fine man. His health . . ."

"Fine," I say, but this is not what she wants to hear, having a keen interest in minor ailments, malignant cancers, and hardening arteries. "Fit as a fiddle," I say.

"Yes, of course, no doubt." She is gathering momentum, building up a relentless pressure that will expend itself in the next question. The minute you begin to squirm, however, she pounces, and so one must keep one's demeanor wholly intact.

"And your mother, poor thing, is there any . . . "

"The same, no change at all, Miss Ruby."

I do not know my mother, and therefore this question is not squirming material, although it is indeed of great interest to the nitty-gritty of Miss Ruby's world. Exactly three months after I was born, my mother suffered a near-fatal automobile accident that left her a complete vegetable in the Cumberland Mental Hospital. I visit her twice a year even though she does not know me and never will; I do not exist for her and, in essence, she does not exist for me. During my visits, I have noticed that she is steadily turning yellow over the years, yellow as summer squash.

"It's tragic is what it is, truly tragic. I was telling Sarah this morning just how tragic your mother really is. Your whole family is probably Jefferson City's one unwritten tragedy."

She is referring to my father now. We have run the gamut of possible information leaks, and soon Miss Ruby will dismiss me for larger game. I barely remember my father. He was a short man with large, capable hands that he often put to use on my bottom for the least domestic infraction. We lived together out in the country and my father used to ropewalk every day across a ramshackle railroad trestle in order to get to the post office more quickly. One day he fell thirty feet onto a slab of Tennessee marble. It was billed as a fluke accident, but even at six I knew the real story. I grew up in Grandfather's house on Dogwood Street.

"Well good to see you, dear. Looking well, very well, considering." Miss Ruby places a finger beside her nose and stands and considers me.

"Yes, quite well. Do stop in on Sarah and me, Elizabeth, we're just two lonely old women in need of company. Stop in anytime between six and eight on Mondays or Fridays. We'd love it."

"Good afternoon, Miss Ruby," I say, but she is stalking away, legs pumping up and down, making a beeline for Ramona Stewart, the local beauty school operator, who is crossing the street in her honey-yellow raincoat. Ramona, like Miss Ruby, is chock-full of tragic insights into our town and they barter them, slyly, between them. Grandfather asserts that the two of them have one foot in the grave, so lost that they exist on sheer deter-

mination, and a certain tenacity to which they adhere their pieces
of information.

I turn onto Dogwood Street, suddenly rich with the crisply-
cool smell of maple trees and dying purple rhododendron. The
white front porches grin and grin from out of the dusk, the
grasses of lawns bristle with a deep green promise. The light
itself writhes in the sky against the horizon, then falls to earth
in beckoning tendrils. Lord! it makes a body feel alive—this is
my home. Yet even here or, rather, especially here, one must
keep one's wits about; danger is everywhere. As a matter of fact,
across the street is the house where my kindergarten teacher,
Miss Nancy—a nice lady, by the way, who would giggle at our
jokes even without the punch line—where Miss Nancy took a
shotgun and blew her brains out right in her own front yard
while half the neighborhood strolled to church on a Sunday
morning. The story goes that she left a note which explained to
the county medical examiner, and to the county, she just couldn't
keep her kitchen floor clean anymore and so bedamned with it.

Suicide is popular in this county and is second only to automobile accidents as a vehicle for unnatural death. It is a clue
that neither I nor my grandfather have overlooked, I assure
you, though indeed it is more than a clue: It is the very reason
we are snipe hunters. Not to be a snipe hunter is to throttle your
own throat day after day, is to be, in a word, a suicide. For if you
don't at least hunt for the snipes, you can never know that the
hole is profoundly empty. You are already dead by your own
hand, you do not exist. The point is to hunt on for *dear life*. All
else is a deadly prank. All others dead pranksters. Grandfather
has pointed out, and I agree, that we two are perhaps the only
living adults in the entire county.

There sits Grandfather's house, encased in a line of poplars
that stand like proud sentinels over a treasure. Timothy will open
the door and Grandfather will step over, peck a kiss on my forehead, his eyes wide and surprised, and he will pretend that I'm
the last person he ever expected to see, as well as the most welcome. Last week I found him on his knees in the study, oiling an
ancient, broken rocking chair, a madman with flying rags and
linseed oil. His eyes watered and he seemed to caress the chair

in his haste: the chair was a message. This was his father's chair, he said, eyes sweating great rounded water, found it at the Salvation Army. I happen to know that Grandfather's father chased him at gunpoint from their home in Dandridge, when my grandfather was fifteen, and they never spoke nor saw each other again.

As soon as I cross the front yard, I can smell it, something gone wrong wafting from the house through the night air. On the porch I can see it, parked inside the garage (where no car is supposed to be) and wedged into the shadows, ticking strangely, like a clock. It is the fat man's Buick.

My Uncle Ashmore is notable for two reasons: he is my father's brother and he is a short and ugly fat man, so fat that his eyes and eyelashes are approximately the same things on his face. After my grandmother's funeral, when I was eight years old, Grandfather stalked home, swallowed a bottle of aspirin, then lay down on my grandmother's bed to die. Uncle Ashmore and Aunt Mildred conducted a series of skirmishes downstairs among the in-laws, everyone laying claim to the land, the house, the kitchen utensils when, finally, Grandfather jumped out of bed, ran downstairs brandishing a piece of firewood, shouting: "I'll break your knave's pate you fatherless son-of-a-saint!" and then Uncle Ashmore retreated, troops in tow, out of the house. Soon thereafter we became snipe hunters by mutual consent.

Timothy answers the door and, immediately, I can see a crisis at hand. With both palms cupping his chin, like a terrified child, he minces back and forth across the threshold. "Lord Lordy!" he says, meaning "trouble." The last time Timothy said "Lord Lordy!" there was three feet of water in the basement and he held a drowned rat in both hands. He stops mincing and comes closer, mouth to my ear.

"Lord Lordy!" he whispers confidentially, then grabs the back of his pants for a steadier stance.

"It's all right, Timothy," I whisper, but he moves quickly up the stairs and disappears. They are in the library down the hall, the fat man's drone welling out from inside. Framed by the library doorway is a ceiling-to-floor case of books that appears to lean uncomfortably against the wall. I have not noticed this before and will certainly attend to it shortly. It would not do to have such a bulk of books collapse upon some innocent passerby.

"Lizzie! I'll be damned"—it is Uncle Ashmore, smiling profusely, his face so swelled I envision his lash-eyes bursting apart to reveal two empty sockets—"Look Mildred, it's Lizzie herself."

"Good evening, Uncle Ashmore, Aunt Mildred." They perch as best they can on a sofa, Tweedledee and Tweedledum grown to mammoth proportion. The sofa visibly sags, and Uncle Ashmore is making quick, furtive glances toward the fireplace. Grandfather sits in his father's chair, rocking it lazily with a thin-lipped smile on his face. In three steps I am beside him, kiss his cheek, then I move off to an easy chair, settling into it.

"Looking real good, gal," Uncle Ashmore says, "just real good. Mildred, just look at our Lizzie, grown right up is what she's done."

"Right up," Aunt Mildred says and studies some difficulty in the hem of her skirt.

"That's just what I say," says Uncle Ashmore. "Lord how time flies," he says, glancing toward the fireplace.

"Time flies," I tell Grandfather and he nods and smiles, thinly.

"What was that?" Uncle Ashmore says. He looks quickly at me and then at Grandfather. "I missed that one," he says.

"I said: 'Time flies.'"

"O yes, it do, indeed it do." The atmosphere is strangely akin to a high-pressure salesroom, Uncle Ashmore looks fit to explode out of his fat-stretched skin, and I notice that this easy chair is much more unyielding than I remember. Aunt Mildred is busy picking strings from her cotton hem.

"Elizabeth," Grandfather says, rocking, "James here has spent the day discussing, what *was* your word, James?—a proposition?—discussing a proposition he and Mildred have come up with."

"O, and what is it?" I ask and turn to look at Uncle Ashmore, who becomes quite red and appears to contemplate assisting Aunt Mildred with her hem.

"It ain't a proposition, never said it was. I'd say it's more like a necessity, practical, I'd say." Amazingly enough, Uncle Ashmore has of a sudden become deeply engrossed in my aunt's hem.

"We're practical people," Aunt Mildred says quickly, not looking up.

"Well what is it?" I ask.

"Well." He rears back and places his hands palm up on his knees in imitation of an honest man from the movies. "You're a smart girl, Lizzie, only person what can talk sense into this old rascal." He pauses, looks shyly in Grandfather's direction, then carefully studies the fingernails of his right hand. Then, as if he can't keep it in any longer, might burst with it, he leans forward: "Sell the house, I say, sell it and let this man rest at last." That said, Uncle Ashmore slaps his knee and returns to his perching position with the facial expression of a man who's just made good sense.

"James wants me to rest at last, Elizabeth, and he wants you to talk sense into me and Mildred, I believe, agrees with James." He keeps rocking, back and up, his smile a tight, thin curve.

"Mildred and me've got it all figured out," Uncle Ashmore says, excitement like the pox all over his face. "We'll do all the organizing for the auction. Get a good price, too, in this neighborhood. Then we'll take this man to a place Mildred and me found in Memphis this summer, most beautiful place you ever saw, weather always fine, 'mongst people with the common interests. You should see the care they take with their people, doctors and checkers and dancing every weekend. Damn near made *my* mouth water. It's what he deserves, too, and about time he got it." Uncle Ashmore has become downright angry with the rush of his own train of thought, and then immediately he becomes bashful, hanging his head, as if such a show of emotion were unbecoming to a grown man. I realize that my hands are somehow driven deeply into the cushions of the easy chair.

"Is that it?" I ask.

"Yes," he says, "except a course the details come later. Now don't it make sense, Lizzie, him here all alone in a house too big for him, you out on your own, and him all alone in this great big house? Don't it make sense?"

"Practical, I'd say," Aunt Mildred says. They both stare at me with whatever lies behind their lashes. Grandfather just rocks, eyes closed and smiling, thinly and tightly smiling.

"Get out of here, please," I say, quite calmly. "Will you both please leave this house, please?"

"Hold on now, Lizzie," Uncle Ashmore says. "This is new and all, think it out, try it on for size."

"Timothy!" I shout and, miraculously, he appears in seconds. I point toward Uncle Ashmore and Aunt Mildred, then toward the library door. "Show my uncle and aunt to the front door, would you."

"Mmm," he says and grins and points a bent arm toward the library door, shuffling up to within inches of Uncle Ashmore's feet.

"Sure," Uncle Ashmore says, loudly. "O sure, we can take a hint." Already Aunt Mildred has teetered to her feet with a sniff and is waddling in the direction indicated by Timothy's finger. "Get one thing straight you, you cash register." Uncle Ashmore flings a hand toward Grandfather, shouting now: "This man's old and incompetent and he's taking that trip west, O yes, law's on my side this time. Talked to a lawyer and I got the court in my pocket. You're all goddamned crazy and the whole town knows it. Hell! that idiot standing there with his arm crooked and his head half gone is enough to prove it."

"Thoroughly enjoyed your visit, James," Grandfather says. "Always remember that my home is your home and do come see us again soon." He stops rocking.

Uncle Ashmore rises to his feet, his breathing harsh, and pushes Timothy roughly aside, apparently digging out from the room a space for himself to breathe.

"Crazy sonsabitches," he says and is gone.

The three of us remain motionless until the sound of the fat man's Buick ticks out of hearing, then Timothy breaks out into an elaborate frown. "Night Lord Lordy," he says and then abruptly we are all laughing, slapping our thighs, hooting an unbroken tattoo of simpleminded hoots. But after a while, we hush.

"Grandfather," I say.

"Elizabeth?" he says.

"I believe I'll fix that bookcase, it looks a trifle unsteady."

"You're right, by God," he says, looking. "It's warped around the edges."

"Grandfather," I say.

"Yes," he says.

"Let's leave it be."

"Yes, of course, we won't touch it. We won't even think it."

And then my grandfather, who will never die, not so long as I live, not so long as the mountains and valleys of East Tennessee live, commences to rock. For we, my grandfather and I, are snipe hunters.

Invictus

amaw's white face broke out of the darkness and hovered like a tear over Leota's eyes. The face bobbed up into the bedroom air, slid down toward the bedpost, then whipped up again into the air and on into the ceiling where it disappeared in gray cobwebs. Sitting up on the bed, Leota opened her eyes and saw the same room, then closed her eyes and, still seeing, lay down on the pillow. Wide-eyed and grinning, Mamaw's face swooped down from the ceiling and fell onto the bedpost, breaking into jagged pieces without a sound.

"Mamaw!" she cried and jerked upright in the bed. Between the close-pressed curtains over the window the early moonlight fell in long pencil strokes, breaking upon the stiff bedposts and the bed's thick footboard, and lay across the white sheets under which Leota's legs quivered and strained like two buried beasts frantic for air. Leota rolled out of the bed and fell onto the floor, pressing her face to the cool wood and feeling the dust grit into the skin as her face slid sideways over its own moisture. Over the edge of the bed the twisted white sheet dripped to a sharp point and hung like an icicle above the floor.

"Are you all right, honey?" Leota's Daddy whispered hoarsely, leaning into the splintered moonlight on the bed.

"I don't feel good, Daddy," she said.

"What's the matter with you?" He dropped a flat palm from the bed onto the back of her neck where it spread out in a wide puddle that inched into her skin deeper and deeper until she felt the coldness at her throat. "Why, you're hot as a firecracker. You get on back in bed and I'll get you a wet washcloth, honey."

He grunted, rising, then padded to the door, the springs of the
bed still squeaking as he walked though the mattress no longer
moved, and he turned at the door, looking back into the room
where now Leota's dark head floated perpendicular to the bed-
side and again said, "You get on back in bed."

"Daddy," she said, "can I get Momma up? She always knows
what to do."

"No," he said. He spoke loudly, his eyes rolling, and quickly
bit his lip slantwise into a knotted scar. "She's, she's asleep in
your room and there ain't no need in us waking her. She wanted
to be alone. She's tired, Leota, you understand that, don't you?"

She nodded. The day had grown cold and rainy and even
then Leota had felt hot as the people crowded in close bunches
under the Colboch-Price tent to keep the water off their hats,
the drops whipping sideways onto their legs and arms. Surrounded by people, the preacher and Mamaw in her brass-edged
box grew bigger until it seemed to Leota that the black derbies
and veils covered miniature dolls weeping into cotton hankies.
The dolls, swallowed in black cloth, hunched in a smooth semi-
circle around the hole; it was a deep square emptiness, heaving
up a thick pile of dirt over the side and into a lump on the ground.
The wind started thin trickles of rock tumbling faster and faster
down the side and into space, sliding soundless into the darkness. Leota knew that God was down there and she turned to
her momma who held her hand in a tight fist, saying, "God is
down there, Momma, and pretty soon they'll drop Mamaw in
with Him and they'll . . . "—but her momma started jerking hard
on her arm and she hushed, though her momma's arm kept
jerking just as hard so that Leota looked up into her face and
saw the whites of her eyes staring straight ahead, the arm still
jerking even after Leota pulled away.

Two weeks before, while she sat cross-legged on her bedroom
floor with dozens of comic books flapping in her lap and perching on her shoes, her momma had poked her head through the
cracked door—the head hung there in space, tilted in the air
like a broken doorknob—and said, "Get your clothes together,
we're going to Mamaw's." Leota looked at her momma and saw
the eyes staring hard into her face, unblinking into the inside of

her head and through her into the wall behind and on outside into the dark mountains that rose and fell in undulating waves of earth.

"Momma?" she asked, the comics fluttering around her.

"Just get your clothes together, you hear me," and the door slammed shut with the sharp clap of loose board on hardwood, the noise louder afterwards. Then the door creaked open again by itself. Pouting down on her comic books, Leota stacked them one by one until a pile leaned sideways on the floor (*Casper* and *Little Lulu* on top, filing on down to the good ones, *Batman* and the *Great Green Hulk*) and she fingered their torn edges, gazing onto the wrinkled pictures and the printing she could not read.

"Don't worry, you can go with me," she whispered. Sad Sack laughed up at her from the top of the pile. Grunting, she scooped the books into her arms and waddled to the dresser, setting them carefully next to her rocks. Along the walls above her bed, wads of silly putty held the bodies of her superheroes, flying and leaping toward the ceiling, some ballooning in overstretched obesity, others pointing in starved flight. Sometimes at night Leota would wake up in bed to find an unstuck Superman, arms outstretched, lying on her covers. Then she would stand up sleepy-eyed on the bed and push the man back onto the wall, certain that he had been flying around and around above her, conquering monsters. She tied a nightgown around her waist, picked up her comics, and staggered from the bedroom with the nightgown scraping behind like a laced tail.

Outside in the den her daddy and her momma faced one another like cats in an alley, moving sideways with eyes slitted and necks averted as if unaware of each other. Leota stepped into the room and peeked from behind the fortification of comics, then stood mouse-quiet, the tail loose on the floor and her back trembling from the weight in her arms.

"I say we can talk this over," her daddy said, keeping his eyes on the television.

"I'm going to mother's," said her momma, her mouth twitching. "I'm sick and tired of your shenanigans. Dear God, Floyd, there's no rest with you. There's just no rest." They stopped circling. Ticking over a couch, the wood-colored wall clock beat in time with Leota's heart and she nodded her head with it, the blood in her ears now.

"Dammit Katie, you want to squeeze me up like some kind of teddy bear." He screwed up wrinkles into his face, the whiskers on his chin sharp as bristles.

"I don't want anything. I just want . . . I'm so tired," she shook her hair and it flowed darkly about her ears, tipping down onto her shoulder, lightly beckoning. Walking over, he placed his arm around her, gently, as if she might shatter into crystal pieces along the dusty floor.

"Let go of me," she screamed, struggling away, "I can't think." Arms still spread, he glanced up in surprise, then in one swoop he whipped around and crashed his fist into the wall, the clock falling onto the couch and lying face up, still ticking. Leota backed a few steps into the hall. Stiff in the legs, her momma teetered over to her daddy and tugged on his sleeve like a small child. Leota stood watching them, her momma pulling and plucking at her daddy's sleeve, her daddy staring with his eyes upraised, and Leota just stood, watching.

"She was the best woman a man ever had," Papaw Jarnegin said, his face so wrinkled that all the blood squeezed into his nose and glowed there like the bulb of a thermometer. Standing rigidly beside the box, his arm draped, almost pasted, onto the shoulder of his neighbor, Papaw talked between his teeth (they slapped in and out of his mouth in short snaps), flicking his tongue along the gray lips. The preacher read on—though he glanced at Papaw, frowning—and poised the fingers of one hand on the box as if to hold it down. "Yessir, there ain't another woman like Katherine to be found in the world. I declare, and I ain't saying this to disrespect the dead, but I just don't think her up and dying on me when I got my Western Union retirement and come home for good for the first time in forty-five years, I don't think that was no accident." Leota looked away onto the square-speckled green hill and onto the line of black cars snaking unbelievably on and on and finally dropping headlong into the earth in the gray distance. She watched her momma stare blindly frontward at the fringed flaps of the parlor tent, great globs of water rolling from her eyes now, then watched her grandfather as he eased a brown cigar from its lining and jammed it unlit into his mouth, still talking: "And she looked out the door real quiet-like and that ain't no big deal but then she said, 'It's getting dark awful early tonight,' but it weren't but three in the afternoon—a sunny day, too, if you remember—then she walked down to the back bedroom and lay down for a nap is what I reckoned but then she died right on that bed, you know, the guest bed. I called the doctor's and he come over with this long-needled thing to give me a shot to calm my nerves because he said in his Yankee whine, 'Yes, I'm afraid your wife has died,' but I wouldn't take no shot. I took my wife's death like a man and that doctor said as much, too."

Leota remembered Mamaw with a popsicle in her hand. Her face white and soft as powder coming to a sharp point at the top of her head, Mamaw high-stepped down the basement steps ("I'm a-feared of rats," she always said and Leota could almost see the dark, furry things swimming in waves of motion on the dry concrete floor) and, holding Leota's hand, lifted the back of the long freezer. Cold steam billowed up and out, white against the strange, dark basement air, then Leota stretched on tiptoe to look into the box. Deep in the corner the popsicles lay side by side in rows, waiting for Mamaw to dip her thin hand into the cold and grab one, giggling, "Bedamned if they aren't getting away," as if they had miraculously sprouted paws and scurried like moles in the darkness, then Leota laughed and Mamaw laughed, giving her a popsicle—orange usually.

Once, when Papaw was coming home on the train, Mamaw grew jittery, forgetting to get the popsicle, and Leota sat in the great old living room, afraid to ask and afraid to creep down the creaking wooden stairs into the black basement. She looked at her comic books, spread in rows on the frayed carpet, peeping at Mamaw who paced in the hallway, up and down, with her hands wringing each other, their blue veins like swollen rivers. In one corner of the basement a huge furnace sat open-mouthed with an orange glow rippling along its lips and Leota knew that it lived and breathed, eating at fat piles of coal and blowing hot breath into the house through crisscrossed grates in every room. The box with the popsicles inside leaned on the wall right across from the furnace.

Rattling at the door and finally flinging it open, Papaw burst into the room carrying brown bags in one hand. Mamaw stopped at the end of the hall, her hands caught in a tight wrestle, then she pattered into the hall, tossed her arms about Papaw's neck in a loose hug.

"You made it!"

"No thanks to Southern Railroad, that's for damn sure," he said, "crazy nigger engineers lickered up and driving down the tracks like maniacs—man's not safe anymore." His nose shone deep purple, but his eyes sparkled and he pecked a kiss at Mamaw's cheek. "Good to see you, Katherine," he said, embarrassed.

"You old fool," Mamaw whispered, "I was worried sick and you out gallivanting with your cronies. I could whip you."

"Well I'm home, Katherine—all's right in the world, ain't it? I'm hungry as a dog, let's eat us something." He dropped the bags, then noticed Leota hunched on the floor, rising like a shadow from her papers. "Why look who's here—little Katie." Hanging her head, Leota plucked at a colorful page corner, wriggling from the attention that quickly shifted into the kitchen.

"By God, I could eat that whole goddamned mahogany table and gnaw the chairs for dessert," he bellowed, echoes knocking into each other down the hall. Clatter and running water sounded from the kitchen and Leota plunged back into her comic books, their pages like mere paper now.

"Leota, honey, come on. We've eaten, but there's still that popsicle a-waiting, isn't there?" Mamaw held out her hand, winking, and Leota jumped to her feet, stepping on the comics—the paper screamed as it crumpled, one page tearing in jagged halves—and ran to her grandmother. On the steps, with the basement door shut behind them, Mamaw pulled Leota close and whispered in her ear, "It's nice having him come home, isn't it?"

"Yes'm." Leota bit into a fingernail and chewed on it, thinking that she would like a grape one this time.

"I have a secret for you, Leota. It's only good when they've gone and come back, you see. The trick is having them gone . . . they can always come back."

Above their heads the rain pattered onto the tent, a drumroll discreetly soft, disturbing no one, yet exciting Leota. Her heart pounded in her head and her feet began marching in time to the rhythm—mud flecking up onto her white ankle socks and onto her bare legs, pink and feverish underneath the brown motes. None of them noticed her. She marched with her legs pumping up and down, up and down until the rain stopped suddenly.

The sun had beat down on Leota's head, high above all the flowing people and, glancing off upper-story windows on the storefronts, spears of light streaked whitely onto the street and thudded in the dust, disappearing. With bare feet placed in the stirrups of Papaw's hands, she rode on his stiff shoulders, knees tucked tight against his neck, and when they stopped at the curb, Papaw reared back, standing at attention, his back stiff so that Leota could drop her hands from his head and watch the parade, rich with the big world she could see at last. Along the sidewalks the grinning show windows of the buildings pushed the crowds of people in heaves onto the street, little boys sprawling stomach-down into the dust, then scurrying frantically back into the wads of human legs and boots, and the horns of the marching bands eased louder, then louder still into the grumbles and cries of hundreds of mouths. Leota watched from her perch, laughing.

Leaning forward, knees tight, she ate peanuts; took them between her teeth, cracked the shell and picked out the nut whole in her mouth, letting the shells fall over Papaw's nose. She cracked the nuts until a mouthful glutted her tongue, then she spat them into her hand, lining the round kernels onto the shining bald crown of Papaw's head, flat and unmoving under her touch.

"Don't move, Papaw," she cried as a few nuts rolled slowly toward the hairs along the sides of his head. Her grandfather stiffened obediently, holding Leota's wriggling toes in a loose grasp. To their right, a man with a great Stetson hat stood with a black bird on his shoulder, the bird squawking in a flutter of collapsing wings. Staring across the street, Papaw watched the little boys, smiling when they hit the dust on their knees. The man with the Stetson looked up at Leota who was peering hard at the bird and he grinned, a roan tooth flickering beside his white teeth.

"Goddammit to hell!" the bird screeched and fluttered against Papaw's shoulder, its beak digging into his coat, sharp as a sliver of glass.

"What?" Papaw bellowed, falling forward, his teeth plopping from his mouth and lying in a grin on the dusty street. "Whad de hell you mean, you son of a bitch?" he blasted toward the man with the Stetson. The peanuts flew into the dust, too, and Leota's face leaned right onto Papaw's nose, her body hunched forward on Papaw's bent back, and she could see the puckered hole of his mouth, caved in at the lips, but still talking: "Whad de hell you mean?" Swooping up, the bird flapped into the air, then came down, onto the far shoulder of the man whose roan tooth gleamed dully now. Bending down and plucking up Papaw's teeth, the man dusted them on his coat and handed them, still grinning, back to Papaw.

"Lord, Lord, I'm sorry, mister," the man said, "you can see hit weren't me, hit's my bird," and he tilted his shoulder to show Papaw. "Goddammit to hell!" the bird blurted again, less loudly, perceiving an audience and leaning forward to stare at Papaw with red-black eyes. Grabbing his teeth, Papaw snarled at the man and pulled out his hankie, swiping the dirt from them and plunging them back into place, quickly, as if life itself could leave a toothless man. The man with the Stetson backed into a wall of people and receded, his bird squawking, into invisibility.

"Look, Papaw, look!" Leota cried, pointing down the street at the prancing, glittering majorettes as they topped a hill and glided smartly toward them.

"Goddammit to hell is right," Papaw muttered. The band followed, drums beating, horns flashing in sharp yellow bullets, legs marching raised high, almost to the waist, and the music—loud, blaring, wonderful to Leota—filled the hot air with jarring rhythm so thick that she could taste it, wanting to hold her ears but listening in exquisite pain. On and on they came—bands in red tunics, green ones, orange ones, and the sound clapped against the storefronts, then raced across to the other side, pounding into those buildings, back and forth and back until it settled into the street, onto the bands, only to be flung back into the quivering buildings. Next came rows of squat antique cars, the men inside tooting the horns and waving, then the crowds quieted, a stillness breezed onto the people, and Leota tugged on Papaw's ear, demanding, "What is it, Papaw, what's wrong?"

"Hush," he said, craning his neck up the road where now a single person marched, slowly, deliberately, his face empty, his hands gripping a huge red and blue flag. Silence hung over the whole town, though wisps of drum cadence drifted like smoke from way in the distance, and the flag hung limp on the pole, its black-crossed lines rippling at the folds, unmoving. In panic, Leota squinted her eyes, watching the lone man, trying desperately to see some magnificence in the limp flag and at last she looked down. After a while lines of men with animals walked past, some dragging monkeys that jerked and slashed at their leashes, some pulling cages on wheels with smiling foxes and flickering squirrels inside. One man marched proudly beside a huge rolling beast—a monster, Leota thought—and it sat up on its haunches, then, flailing thick, black paws, it squatted in front of the crowds. The little boys cheered, then pushed one another toward the animal, scaring themselves when they found the thing rising furry and dark close by and they dove like fish back toward the sidewalk, mouths gaping in terror.

"By God," Papaw said, lifting his eyes to Leota, "that's Earl Dickey's dog. The old coot's passing the thing off as a bear. I declare, they ought to leash him up and parade him down the street. Does look like a bear, though, must've lost his tail in a dogfight." The last of the parade skipped out of sight, into the redness of the sunset down the street, and Leota, tired into her bones, rode Papaw toward the car.

In front of her, six men (Papaw was there) picked Mamaw up and carried her to the hole, puffing as they lowered her into the blackness. Black figures trailed out from the tent, their heads blossoming into huge umbrellas though it no longer rained, and Leota grabbed her momma's hand once more. Turning dead eyes on her, her momma squeezed both hands terrifically onto Leota's pale face and pulled her close to her mouth, whispering in a low, savage voice, "It will be like this. It will be black as a pit from pole to pole." Leota struggled free with a cry and backed away, her heart throbbing like that of some wild animal, caged and tamed for years yet suddenly remembering its freedom, but her momma stood motionless, still bent over with her hands cupping round nothing now and her open mouth silent, though wide.

"Here you go, honey, this will cool you off some," her daddy said and he patted the rolled washcloth onto her forehead. She winced as the cold gripped the top of her head, slamming her brain against the inside of her eyes, then the cloth warmed and finally grew hot so that she tossed it onto the floor where it splattered on the wood and lay like a fat worm inching toward the door. Her daddy's arm curved on Leota's pillow, the blue eagle on his bicep stretched longways, gripping a pink scroll with the word KATIE contorted almost into an unrecognizable scribble. He slept with his mouth open and snored hot breath onto the side of her face. Along the pillow his arm relaxed and slid lower and lower until it rested heavily on her head and his face lolled closer so that his nose nudged at her ear, the breath steaming her skin. She lay stiff on the bed.

"Momma," she called, too softly for hearing, unsure even that she opened her mouth. "Momma, Momma." They had stood in the kitchen (Papaw had brought them home from the funeral in the retirement Cadillac, proudly showing Leota all the buttons and knobs, her momma silent and unmoving in the back), while her daddy frowned with clenched fists and her momma drooped with eyes open fixed on the floor and Leota watched with bottom pressed tightly into the dark corner next to the stove. From the faucet fat streams of water cried into the sink, then gurgled down the drain, and now it sounded like an old or crippled wild beast dropped incredibly there to drink in the act of dying. Leota had shivered from an awful prehension of the scene and she leaned on the walls, not afraid but curious, as if only her head and not her body crouched invisible against the shadows.

"What's the matter with you?" her daddy had asked her momma, Leota all but unborn in their minds. "You've got to pull yourself together, woman." Pounding onto metal, the water beat into Leota's head, driving thick jell against her ears and nose and eyes so that she plugged two fingers into her ears to hold it in and then there was quiet.

"Do you hear me?" he yelled and his fists yanked up to his neck, feinting. "I can't stand this anymore, oh dear Lord, I can't stand this anymore," then his fists loosened and he stood, pressing his palms together in spasms, the fingers alive and trembling. Her momma stared at him. No noise for a while though heat clouded the room, Leota sweating into her Sunday dress, and her daddy's eyes broadened and narrowed, almost like fists opening and shutting. Shambling slowly around, her momma stumbled to leave the room and again his eyes narrowed and broadened; without moving he seemed to jump sharply upright. "Don't you dare leave this room," he yelled again and the words hung in the air like fruit left rotting on the tree. She kept walking. Leota saw only the two forms as they hit the floor, her momma on the bottom, her daddy on top, slapping and slapping her face as if his hand were a whip and her momma's face expressionless as it rocked except for ugly purple-red blotches that deepened, thick and swollen. Breathing hard, her daddy stood up at last and, throwing her momma over his shoulder, he carried her though the kitchen, down the hallway, and into Leota's bedroom, slamming the door. Neither ever saw Leota hidden in the corner. Only that night, when she lay asleep under the sheets alone in her parents' bedroom, did Leota spring reborn into their world as her daddy crept into the bed, saw her lying there, kissed her cheek, and fell to snoring in great heaves into his pillow.

"Momma," she whispered, "oh Momma." The bedroom seemed to spin around the light bulb in the middle of the ceiling, blurring the walls, the bedposts, the moonlight into a gray wash that oozed onto the floor. Sinking deeper into the bed from the weight of her daddy's arm, Leota breathed faster, afraid she would drown in the melting room, her blood boiling from the heat and throbbing at her ears until she cried, "Momma!" louder this time. The dark figure rustled in the bedroom doorway with the soft crackle of silk petticoats and Leota sat upright on the bed, peering into the blackness until the figure moved closer swiftly, its fleshless face glowing whitely in a wide-eyed grin, its arms outstreched, and Leota, almost with relief, saw that it was Mamaw.

South of the Border

I n a car, headed point-blank down an interstate, there is a
sanity akin to recurring dreams: you feel as if every moment has been lived and will be lived exactly according to
plan. Landscapes and peripheral realities blur and rush
headlong backwards through the windows like the soft edges of
sleep. And the road ahead and behind you becomes a straight
line, framed in the perfect arc of a dashboard.

My sister sits hunkered against the side of the car and fiddles
with the radio, careful not to touch my right leg. On a Sunday
morning in the midlands of South Carolina all radio stations
play either gospel music or black church services. Jane Anne
chooses a church service and claps her hands, eyes closed, to the
hiccupping rhythm of the preacher, both his voice and her per-
cussion sounding disembodied in the smallness of the Volkswagen. "Take Jesus, oh Lord take Jesus," the preacher says, "take
Jesus for New Year's." Clap clap clap goes my sister, clap clap.
"Jesus is my friend" clap "Jesus is your friend" clap "Friends,
accept Jesus" clap clap. Deep in her bowels she is a fundamen-
talist, a lover of simple truths and literal facts; her resolution for
the coming year is "to see things more clearly." In this she is
resolute, commenting often on points of interest as we careen
northward through cotton fields and marshy bottomland and
stark-colored advertisements.

I have no such resolution. While driving I develop an acute
myopia and it is all I can do to concentrate on the pavement that
blears and dashes like water underneath the car. Outside the
world flashes by as if switched on and off in a two-dimensional
slide show, one frame at a time, the whole universe condensed
to a television screen.

"Look at that!" Jane Anne cries and points frantically somewhere outside. "Look, look!"

"What was it?"

"You didn't even look," she says. She claps her hands together with a violence that means she wishes one of them was mine. "Didn't even goddamn look at what I saw. You probably had something more important on your mind, I'm sure, probably aren't even interested in that cow I just saw with the human face."

"You just saw a cow with a human face?"

"No," she says, almost happily, "I didn't see a thing," and then she stares sullenly out her window.

Just last night my father and stepmother engaged in a domestic catfight over this kind of optical delusion. During a television football game, the Gator Bowl in Florida, they break out in an almost-brawl over forces beyond their control, forces five hundred miles to their south. Clemson, a South Carolina school, and Ohio State are playing and my father perversely roots for Ohio, a state that exists for him only during television football and basketball games. My stepmother was raised in the thick of Clemson patriotism, a twitch at the corner of one eye blossoming into a full-blown spasm, possibly hindering her vision, at every Clemson penalty and first down.

By the end of the game tension is extreme, my stepmother's eye winks rapidly, my father's mien settles like concrete as he stares at a commercial. Clemson is winning, my palms are sweating and slick, my stepmother is exalted, and my father steadily slips into a familiar attitude. Once, eight years ago, he almost hit me when I won a Monopoly game. His is a competitive madness that operates at a slow boil until all is lost, then his expression explodes into a kind of pseudo-apocalyptic blitz. So when a Clemson player intercepts a key Ohio State pass and Woody Hayes, ex-coach of Ohio State, smacks the Clemson player in the face, my father blitzes out, saying "Kill him, kill the bastard, Woody." My stepmother blithers to her feet (they sit in identical easy chairs, separated by a coffee table), winks and gasps, arms akimbo and shivering, shouting now:

"You might as well say 'kill me' that's what you mean!"

Blitz over, my father settles back into concreteness while my stepmother marches, footstep-echoes beating into the walls against one another, into their bedroom. An hour later everyone is sleeping heavily and even the television has sunk into a blank stupor. Today she poked her head in my bedroom doorway, flashing a smile birthed and bred in South Carolina and cultivated like white cotton, and told me goodbye before she left for church. She plays the organ for the Methodist Church of Fort Motte.

Jane Anne points out advertisements for the South of the Border tourist complex still an hour and a half in the future. CONFEDERATE FOOD YANKEE STYLE, BEST IN THIS NECK OF THE WOODS one sign reads. So frequent are these advertisements that they serve as punctuation along the sameness of the interstate and I begin to despise them because I feel my utter dependence on their familiarity. I come South twice a year, once at Christmas, once in the summer, each time more of an amnesiac experience than the visit before. I am fearful that after another few visits I may go home and never be able to leave, my present and future eradicated by the vicious tenacity of the past. But, truly, I am hypnotized home by the staid reality of what I remember— a somnambulatory reality so familiar and so unchanging that it appears to be the only true god in my life.

"I'd be a fool to stick around," Jane Tressel sings from the radio. My sister has found an AM station. Lips taut and round, she sings along with her mouth forming the words as if molded around an ice-cream cone. The way she sings turns the words into nonsensical baby-noise, but this is also a special function of AM radio, this ablution of meaning into a catchy anonymity. Jane Anne carefully reads several beauty magazines, pining over the structured perfection of the models, always running out to buy new beauty products although she is as frugal with her money as a squirrel in autumn. A stranger, she sits so close to her door that no place in the car could be equally far from me and she eyes the side of my face with the wariness of a stray dog. She could be a nervous hitchhiker, except that she controls the radio. This trip is the first time we have been together alone in eight years. She is a stranger, stranger still because for thirteen years we slept in the same bedroom and now she resembles a kewpie doll rather than a younger sister.

With her left hand, when it is not spiraling around the radio tuner, Jane Anne tosses boiled peanuts between her lips. They look like a pile of swelled ticks, gray-skinned and blood-bloated, in the palm of her hand, and she is soberly emptying a paper sack full of them. I have noticed that she eats in a dazed trance, similar to the manner in which she sings to the radio, as if eating were a habitual duty. She was always a dutiful child, and now she weighs one hundred and seventy-five pounds, has a prematurely stooped back, and the corners of her mouth pucker down in a perpetual expression of bad humor. An unhappy kewpie doll.

Fifteen years ago she was a beautiful, dutiful child. Fifteen years ago I would bring her red and purple ribbons, watch her thread them through her hair. It looked like miniature maypoles, and when she tossed a braid I wanted to grab one and swing out. Today she wears a mud-colored scarf tied tightly at the nape of her neck.

"Why don't you ever talk seriously to me?" she asks and I grip the wheel, staring hard at the car in front of me, abruptly aware of the scores of vehicles swarming the interstate ahead and behind me. Each one is a possible fatal accident.

"What do you want to talk about?" I say warily, my thighs beginning to feel cramped in the immobile space-time of the traveling Volkswagen interior. In the event of an accident, all is lost in a Volkswagen.

"What do you want to talk about?" Jane Anne mimics in a voice that, remarkably, is more like my own than my own sounds to me. She is full of surprises, this sister of mine whom I do not know. "I'll tell you one damn thing," she says, really angry this time, her tongue flailing against a stray peanut, "you may be smart, but I have all the common sense in this family." Snorting, she clings to the side of her door.

This is true. She does have the common sense in our family, a fact uttered and re-uttered by my paternal grandmother who likens me to my Uncle George Wilkins. My Uncle George was so smart, she says, that he was almost an idiot. He died with a moonshine-ruined liver and a cancer that ate from his breast right through to his back, and Grandmother said it would have gone on through the bed and into the hospital linoleum if his heart hadn't stopped first.

He was a geologist and forever poking rocks with his cane, head bent forward, arm flicking, cane flicking, eyes pouncing toward the ground to examine and file away every square inch of land that his feet passed over. Once he broke his nose against a haybaler, never saw it, saw only the gray-black pieces of sedimentary rock that flipped over and under the tip of his cane. But he was a smart one, my Uncle George, and twice a year scientists from Washington came down to sober him up and fetch him back to a laboratory where he performed penetrating geological studies. They wanted him to fly up there, but he always said he did his traveling on the ground. Now he's his own specimen, buried under six feet of sand and sedimentary rock in Calhoun County, South Carolina, and he's not going anywhere.

"I'll tell you another damn thing," Jane Anne says and warms up to one of our childhood wrangles, the kind where neither of us is aware of the reason but both of us will stake our lives on a resolution in our favor. It is our father's blood that swells up at these times, bubbles of madness that break at the mouth. "I'll miss your sweet, sweet eyes," Willie Neal croaks from the radio, "I told you when I left, I couldn't live with your lies."

"I'm sick and tired of you making me feel stupid. You act like I'm still eleven years old, like I'm still your devoted and moronic pawn. I'm nineteen, damn you, I've read Sartre and Camus." She utilizes her French education in all arguments, since I have studied only Latin and vaguely remember it anyway—French is her code language through which she can curse me to my ignorant face. "I've seen Chicago and New York, I've seen Paris and *you* don't even have a passport."

"A passport isn't exactly a rite of passage, Jane Anne."

"Not," she says, "if you don't even have one." Furious now, she sputters like a cat and is just seconds away from a serious assault. Sometimes when we were younger we'd forget what we were angry about in the middle of a wrangle, and so kept on with it anyway, only louder and with more passion.

"Not," she says, "if you travel with your heart incognito like a goddamn ghost. You've been just a barrel of laughs for two weeks."

"Didn't come down here," I say, grim as a soldier, "in order to entertain my family." There is a white Pontiac endangering my rear bumper.

"Then why, in God's name, did you come at all?" Jane Anne kicks the peanut sack; the Pontiac veers to the left and passes safely, though in a glance I can tell that the man inside it is a lunatic.

"I know one thing and don't you forget it: I am as educated as you are, I am as competently conversive as you are."

This, too, is true. In fact, Jane Anne can shift facilely between Sunday dinner chatter at my grandmother's and mournful sympathetico at my aunt's where my first cousin, Jonathan, is dying of cancer. Both situations strike me dumb.

At my grandmother's Christmas dinner, I deaf-mute my way through the awkward vacuum during which butt-pinching uncles watch football games and bouffant-headed aunts question me as to how many boyfriends I have and my grandmother pounces at odd moments to bark in my ear, "Can't go to school forever!" Normally I wink and grin like a demon, offer condolences for my slovenly personality, giggle madly while my butt is tweaked, and create countless football players who appear and disappear as boyfriends according to my whim. Once I created a rather bookish law student who was poorly received and he disappeared during the course of dessert, an hour later reappearing as a dashing quarterback who was a well-received pre-med. This time, however, I sleepwalk, staring maniacally at each relative until they leave me alone.

"Time to eat!" Grandmother cries, pertly, her presence in its element and as relentless as a Mack truck. Fourteen grown men and women rise as one and throng into the kitchen where dishes of food, festive-colored and bubbling, are lined in perfect rows to be picked over, placed on china plates and retired to the dining room, there to be consumed in dutiful silence. But first comes the continuum in which fourteen grown men and women hang back, hem-haw, pluck at their sleeves or pick their noses, succumb to the cowardliness of not being first in line though for five hours their appetites have been titillated to the peak of a savage desire. For a few seconds we stand like tame vultures and just peer, ravenous, at the untouched food. I believe I will faint from hunger, until I finally find myself at the table, slapping mashed potatoes onto crisply cool china.

"Jane Anne," Grandmother says in her grand commandeering tone, a tone reminiscent of both grade-school teachers and Methodist preachers, "would you please say grace." Jane Anne positively glistens with glee, jubilant while all eyes pin me against the profaned table, potatoes puffed and accusing on my plate.

"For these Thy gifts, Oh Lord let us be thankful," Jane Anne croons, in a strangerly fashion. The surge is on now, compliments and condiments fly across the table, and I sleepwalk through dinner, an attendant to disapproval.

FREE IN-ROOM MOVIES: TWENTY HONEYMOON SUITES I read on a huge sign. In twenty minutes we will pass through the middle of South of the Border, almost into North Carolina. The peanuts have risen once more into Jane Anne's lap, and she nimbly eats them. "It's my last night in town, I'd be a fool to stick around," the radio says. I do not know the performer although his song is appealing in its drowsy insistence. At South of the Border Jane Anne will meet a boyfriend from her school and I will continue north to my school alone. Both of us are hyper-aware of the advertisements, as if they are motes of sand trickling time away. She wants to get out of my presence as badly as I do hers; we are both morbidly afraid of each other. FREE—ADVICE, AIR, WATER. EVERYTHING ELSE REASONABLE.

"Another thing," she says, wrapping up her side of the dialectic before handing the floor to me, "you have been nothing but rude and ill-mannered this whole vacation, to me, to Daddy, even to Aunt Louise. You lack discrimination, that's what you lack."

"Jonathan . . . how is he?" Jane Anne whispers to my aunt. I perch on the lips of a couch, finger wringing finger, my tongue thick as a marble tombstone.

"Dying," my aunt chokes, "dy—ing."

"How long?" Jane Anne looks absolutely engrossed, a dutiful child.

"Days, weeks, God knows when he'll be free from the pain." Solemnly Jane Anne acknowledges the mercy of God with a slow, dazed nodding of her chin. She is gathering momentum for the predictable eventuality wherein my aunt will begin to sob and she can console with a firm and warm arm across the heaving back. But—surprise—my aunt visibly marshals her circumference and pulls herself together with a prolonged sigh. My palms are clammy with the dead and the living.

"Sarah Louise is home," my aunt says, giddy with recovered strength, but poised along some precipice of mental breakdown. Sarah Louise is also my first cousin. "She's in the back bedroom getting dressed." Sarah Louise is in the back bedroom getting dressed, Jonathan is in the front bedroom, blinds drawn, dying. For a while we sit in an uncomfortably loud silence until Sarah Louise comes into the living room. Like her mother, Sarah Louise has reddish-brown hair and a pointed face that articulates itself at the breach of the nose. She looks like a rumpled domesticated animal, exhaustion whitening her cheeks in random places like frostbite. She is looking directly into my eyes.

"He wants to see you, Bo."

"Me?"

"He's asking for you."

Jane Anne shivers and recoils, I recoil, a creeping nausea deep inside my throat; I wish to hell I was somewhere, anywhere, somebody someplace else. When I was two, Jonathan christened me into the family by nicknaming me Bo, a name used only by blood relatives and, to them, a name coincidental with my very existence. Only recently has Jane Anne begun to call me Jennifer, her statement of self-determination. Nomenclature is her forte.

I remember Jonathan in two ways: first, the way he looked at eleven, knobby-kneed and skinny as a fence post, my best friend and comrade. Like rabid dogs we chased the cows on his father's farm until they ran idiotically into their pond water and grouped together up to their buttocks in sludge and cattails. The days I spent with him were always warm and cloudless and kinetic with revelry. We played doctor inside the very room where he now lies dying; he was the first man I ever studied. Once my father found us together and beat me with a leather belt until welts crisscrossed my bare legs and back like textile woof. Afterwards, since we lived in different towns, he grew out of revelry and into proms and long-legged cheerleaders. I saw him last two years ago, a young man so handsome he could send pangs of romance down the back of Ayn Rand herself. Blond hair feathered and long around his neck, the face of a beautiful woman made a little rough at the edges, an unaware body oozing casual strength and grace, the man was unbearably pretty. I believe the mythic Christ, aided by centuries of imagination, could never approach the fullness of reality in Jonathan's splendor.

I stand and rub my hands together and they slide against their own moisture. In times of stress I enter into a semicomatose state like an instinct-driven opossum. Automatically my brain begins to decline a Latin noun, a ae ae am a, ae arum is as is. The room is shadowed and unlit, a thickly-queer smell of medicine and urine and *sweet Jesus* the smell of life itself condensed into a pungent and rancid death-room, without light and without hope. I feel an acute hatred for myself, sweat trickling—an endless beading health—under my armpits: da ta ta ta, a ae am a, this is the way the world ends. Across the room the bed seems to rest against the far wall but surely to God he is not in it, there is no indentation under the quilt, there is only a skull resting on the pillow, a yellow hairless sunken skull.

"Bo," he says, a muffled, anonymous sound, drugged, removed, a physical impossibility save in nightmare. Dipping strangely, the lines of the room combat with a nausea, and I realize my mouth is whimpering and salivating. This nausea moves around the throat like unconscious prayer. The sting is for the da ta ta ta, arum is as is.

"Bo," he whispers, "I wanted to tell you . . . "

"Tell me."

"It's not so bad."

"Tell me quick."

He coughs without coughing, resting. Two more minutes and I will go mad and this thought is comforting. Someone is whimpering somewhere.

"Are you still my friend?"

("Fucking Jesus!" Jonathan yells and punches the air with his fist. The cowshed blows up in slow motion, splinters of wood fall like dust on his hair and shoulders. Large pieces of board fly over the fence, landing with dull thuds in the pasture. Down below, huddled up and frightened, Bo studies the delicate white hairs on the back of his right leg.)

"I wanted to tell you goodbye," he says.

(The others said, "Don't tiddle in the pond," but they pay no attention. They are full, with the warm brown water pressing against them, and they pay no attention. Across the water, stabbed by erect cattails, the cows stand knee-deep and black near the pond's edge, tails slapping onto their backs, heads browsing onto the surface then easing back up to stare at pine trees. Bo and Jonathan know that they think of great things, standing there in the water, staring. They tiddle freely and silently into the pond.)

"It's not so bad," he says.

I pretend I haven't heard.

"It leaves."

"Jonathan . . . "

"Goodbye," he says. "I loved you, yes," and then he starts to doze.

"Goodbye."

I return to the living room and begin to cry. My aunt and Sarah Louise begin to cry. Jane Anne stares at me with narrow eyes, her mouth puckered in distaste, then she pats and coos and comforts Sarah Louise. Uncontrollably I want to punch her in the nose, kiss her on the mouth, dash outside to the car, and get the hell out of South Carolina. A past is dying out from under my feet and I notice for the first time the blinking red lights on my aunt's Christmas tree. One two three, one two three they waltz, immobile, on the outskirts of the fir needles. I picture my sister wrapped in red lights, clapping her hands—one two three. When we get into the Volkswagen, she says: "You should have controlled yourself, you shouldn't have cried in front of them. We were guests in their house."

Ramona Stewart sings: "The sun's falling from the sky and night ain't far behind." Jane Anne waits for my defensive remarks, contemplating her retort through a wriggling at the lips, the worrying to death of a boiled peanut at the tip of her tongue. "Sun's falling," Ramona goes on, "night ain't far behind."

"Listen, Jane Anne," I say, glancing briefly in her direction, then staring straight ahead, a cheap power play although my hands and eyes are truly busy. She is filing away the information, noting the brevity and attributing it to arrogance.

"Can't we part as friends, can't we please just forget our old roles and part as friends? Please?"

Up ahead a huge sombrero sits atop a five-story tower. We have arrived at our connection, South of the Border. My sister sits in complete silence, one of her half-dutiful trances, and I pull off at the exit and enter the parking lot of a coffee house that is partly Mexican, partly southern, and mostly middle-American slough. Jane Anne's friend slumps manfully against the wheel of a red Datsun hatchback with Wisconsin plates and, suddenly businesslike, Jane Anne is out of the car, suitcase in hand, pocketbook slung in a noose around her neck.

"Goodbye," she says and is gone. I watch while she situates herself in the Datsun, then I pull out of the parking lot, drive up the entrance ramp to the interstate, alone inside the throbbing, hurtling Volkswagen, then insert myself into the welter of anonymous northbound vehicles.

I can go home again, again and again, each episode like a snowflake that sticks to your eyelashes. They melt and mingle with your tears. Take a memory, any memory, and it becomes an inviolable god, a sanity exactly according to plan. But those soft edges—those peripheral realities that blur, those landscapes that shift and rush past—those are the crucibles of emotion, and they flow headlong backwards beneath your feet. I come South only twice a year, once at Christmas, once in the summer. Each time is a possible fatal accident.

Broken Mirrors

Through the sheer living room curtains, across the leaf-strewn yard, Oredia could see the pickup truck. The man inside it was just a bent shadow, but she knew what he looked like: red-eyed and probably crying, hair grown down to his brows, a cigarette plugged tightly into his mouth. When they first married, Harold had been an erect, beautiful man with close-cropped hair and a sliver of mustache above his lips. A good catch, her sister had told her.

The pickup drove past the house again, moving slowly down the street, its red paint a beacon of unsuppressed anger for all the neighborhood to see. At the bottom of the hill he would pull into a driveway and turn around and climb the hill once more, up and back, hovering in front of the house like a stray dog that'd been fed, then whipped, and still couldn't leave the vicinity. Maybe he was lost, had forgotten why, out of all the houses and neighborhoods and towns in Tennessee, he chose to haunt the periphery of this one. Even his face, when she saw it, had the distorted look of a beaten child, as if somehow the world had outgrown him and cast him off with a rude kick in the back.

"Go away," Oredia said, "just go away," and she popped her hand against the arm of her chair. Motes of dust eased up around her fingers.

There had been no peace since they separated, and Oredia could foresee no peace when the divorce came through. The truck would bounce back and forth across her picture window for the rest of her life, its rhythm choreographed to her heart-beat until her very blood would shift gears with the pickup. Even Sheba had begun to sit at her bedroom window, watching her father pass. The child doodled on a sheet of paper (lopsided little drawings of stick people, hollow-eyed ghosts with vacant grins, houses with broken windows, six-legged animals, ravenous fires that ate away at mountainsides), picking up her head as the red machine went past, then doodling some more. At times Oredia made plans to shutter her daughter's windows, to block and protect her from the sight, but the vision of Sheba alone, walled up and alone, stopped her.

Oredia watched the truck ease by once more, then she stood up and pushed down on her skirt with the palm of one hand. She couldn't keep the wrinkles out of her clothes anymore. They cropped up on her blouses and slacks like tiny ringworms, indelible, living creases that covered her body and multiplied. In a few years they would spread to her face and hands and she would be an old woman. Just two months ago she had felt young and lovely, brilliant, unfettered, but that was before she left her family, before she came back. Now she was growing older, and autumn pressed on her mind like the layers of dead leaves in her yard. Soon the trees would be bare and skeletal, a cold wind would whip across the mountains and catch itself in the valley, cradling snow in its wake, winter would come and life—trees, animals, grass—would pretend to be dead.

"Sheba," she yelled, her words sounding harsh, staccato. "Sheba, come here."

They needed eggs and milk and butter. And she'd buy Sheba something sweet, a gingerbread man from the bakery. How gloomy the child was, how abnormally quiet and strange. Oredia wondered what she would think of this skinny, frowning thing, what she would say to her if they were strangers and unrelated. "Smile, little girl," she would tell her, "smile and tell me that you're happy, God loves all the little children." Red and yellow, black and white, loves them all.

"Mama?" Sheba said, her face a question mark that trailed down to the dot of her mouth. Curls of hair, swirling and beckoning on her head, reached onto her forehead and pointed downward to where her eyes gaped wide and green. In her hand, fingers clenched, nails white, she held a black crayon and a sheet of drawing paper.

"Let's see what you're coloring."

"It ain't very good," she said, backing away. The crayon looked like a half-concealed weapon in her hand, an intimation of dark secrets or dark thoughts.

"Let's see it anyway."

Sheba stared at it, pulled it close to her eyes, then shoved it arm's length away, squinting at it. Finally, she held it out between two fingers and her mother plucked it, like an insect, from her hand. In awkward lines she had drawn an easel, and on the easel was a painting of a ramshackle barn, a stark replica of a water-color Oredia had done a year ago and had given to friends.

"This is very nice, Sheba. I didn't think you remembered my painting."

"It ain't anything," Sheba said. "It's ugly," and she held out her hand, her eyes looking straight into Oredia's, or behind them, because there was no recognition glinting in their greenness. Oredia gave Sheba the drawing.

"Listen, honey. I'm going out for a minute. You'll be okay till I get back?"

"Where are you going? When will you come back?" Sheba said, abruptly, at once, as if her mother might disappear into the living room floor. She stood, paper wavering, eyes open like trap-doors, and waited stiffly for an answer.

Phillip was his name, Phillip Langston Chesaton, a grand artist's name for a mediocre painter. Oredia believed she fell in love with the name first, the arrogance next, and the slender body still later. He was married, unhappily, to an acne-pocked woman whose hands—withered, brittle—cooked and cleaned and supported her man, her artist, like humble, selfless crutches. Phillip would tell her, when they met in secret after his water-color classes: "She's constructed of wood and cardboard, witless and passionless, but I've loved her simply because I am her life. Isn't that a hell of an out, loving a woman simply because she denies her own existence? Now you, you I could be *in love* with, you I could share my life with." His life not hers, Oredia knew even then, but she was in love, so in love with an artist that she felt her blood and strength commingled with his.

So she left with him one night on a whim (he had promised Europe and knowledge, happiness forever after), jumped into his jeep and drove off into the night, shoving her husband and her child into the back places of her mind. They got as far as Nashville, and then Oredia saw Sheba, with a clarity akin to dreams, curled up on her bed while her father ranted through the house, breaking things, roaring, cow-like, in a hazy, helpless pain. And Sheba just sat there—what did she think, what could she possibly think?—with her little wan face drawn together in miserable confusion. The sight was too wrenching for Oredia, all the ecstasies of freedom deflated into the hollow of her stomach. Four days later, in Phoenix, she told Phillip to take her back, that she'd die without Sheba.

"If I take you home," he had said, "don't count on seeing me again. I'm not some yo-yo like your husband."

"Take me back."

"He'll probably kill you, you know. Can't be too sure about those working types. He's absolutely rabid by now."

"I want to go back." How she hated men then, all of them. How she hated a world that would permit them their licenses, their petty deceits, their perverse wills and their strengths, their brutish physical strength. He parked at a restaurant in Amarillo and she called home, her hatred a hard stone inside her.

"Harold, it's me," she told the phone.

"Reta, oh Reta!"

"I'm coming back; I can't do this."

"Reta," he said, sobbing. His voice sounded like the broken reverberations of an entombed echo. "Reta, come back, for God's sake come back, come back to me."

"I'm coming back," she said, again, recoiling from his voice as if slapped by it.

"I'll make—I'll make you some coffee, sweetheart, I'll have some coffee ready when you come. Please come back, Reta, God come back."

"I'm coming back. I'll be there in three days."

"I'll have some coffee for you, would you like that? Some coffee . . . " But she hung up, her stomach tight, squeezing her breath into gasps, and walked toward the jeep.

"It's all right, Sheba," she said. "I'm just making a quick stop at the store. I'll bring you a surprise. Would you like a surprise?"

"Yes, Mama." Her stiff shoulders never relaxed, her eyes blinked and squeezed at Oredia's own sadness. Lately, Sheba had had bad dreams, wakening Oredia. She must dream of horrible things, Oredia thought, because her face and hands grew sweaty, as if her body wrung the very salt of her innocence into tiny beaded droplets along its flesh.

"Poor Sheba, come here," Oredia whispered, holding out her arms.

"I'm all right, Mama." She backed away, eyes darting back and forth across the room. "I'm all right."

"I love you very much, Sheba, you know that, don't you?"

"Yes'm."

She just stood and waited, watching her mother's hands drop to her sides. And Oredia sighed, felt old and wrinkled. Pressing her palms upon her skirt, she smiled at Sheba, then turned, gathered up her purse and checkbook, and left the house through the back door. In her car she waited for the truck to pass, to move on down the hill. She started the engine and pulled out of the driveway, heading in the opposite direction.

"I'm sorry, Sheba," she told the rearview mirror, and she watched her eyes succumb to the darkness of their dilating pupils.

Sheba sat in her bedroom, drawing, carving the lines of a tree with black crayon onto white paper, and she glanced through her window in time to see the pickup truck with her father, a crooked gray shape inside it, drive past the house.

"She ain't here," Sheba said, coloring in the trunk of the tree. "She ain't never here. You just," and now she stabbed a bird's nest onto a bare branch, "you just get on home, Daddy. She ain't here."

In her dreams, if she ate a green crayon, she could fly, soaring above the whole town, and people looked like little pinkie fingers, all puffed up and proud in their pretty clothes. When she ate a blue crayon, she came back down to earth, sometimes in a beautiful land, but usually in her own bed. Tonight she could watch television and stay up late. First, the girls in golden costumes made funny pictures with their bodies, dancing, then the four grown-ups came on, shouting and frowning at each other, but always happy in the end. They were the best part, those four grown-ups, and they made her laugh. On television nights Sheba

had her best dreams. On school nights she dreamed of monsters
and ghosts and old men with long pointed noses. If the church
chimed eleven and she was still awake, Sheba would cry because
everyone in the world was asleep, except her, and she might see
something. Those were the nights the old man came to her, his
puckered face grinning madly above her bedpost, his fingers
weaving spiderwebs across her face, and she woke up with her
mother sitting beside her on the bed. Her mother always accompanied the old man.

The old man reminded her of Mr. Miner, the way his nose
shot out like a long tongue from the middle of his face. Every
year Mr. Miner would cut off the heads of snakes he found
winding their way into his yard from the mountain. With the
care of a jeweler, he'd take his shovel and slice the necks of the
copperheads, then he would laugh at Sheba as the headless snakes
contorted in the grass. "Careful," he'd yell, suddenly, grinning,
yelling though she stood yards from him and from the snakes.
"They still got the poison even without their bodies. You'd swell
up and pop from it, like a fat yellow balloon, you'd pop. Bang!"
And then he laughed again, rubbing his belly.

Sheba loved the mountain; the snakes never bothered her.
When her mother had disappeared, she went onto the mountain for half of the night and she was safe there with the stars
that shut on and off, the crickets that shut on and off. She was
not safe at home that night. Her father was not her father and
her mother was gone, vanished, like her dreams, and the old
man was her father and she was awake and her mother was with
that man.

"That man!" her father had screamed. "She's left me for that
man. She's destroyed me for that—that fucking man!" He pranced
up and down the living room in his bare feet—socks, he wore
socks, and his bare big toe poked out from a hole in one of
them—saying, "I'll kill him, I'll kill her and him, then me." Sheba
watched him, her back tight against the cushions of a couch, her
throat so small she breathed through her mouth. For a second
she thought her father looked like a fretful baby, but afterwards
he became a very old man, his nose and eyes and mouth pulled
to one side of his face, all twitching. And then, bellowing, he
rushed to the front door, flung it open, and ran into the yard in

his socks. Sheba jumped from the couch and hurried to the curtains, parting them with two fingers as if they might soil her hands. Outside, her father was running up and down the street, white socks flashing, and his mouth hung open, though she could hear no sounds. After a while he came back inside, walked straight into the living room, his back queerly bent forward; then he flopped on the floor, crying, thrashing against the wood. The bottoms of his socks were dirty. But he cried so loudly, his face an unrecognizable pinkness, that Sheba left the house and climbed her mountain where it was safe, where she could breathe through her nose and let her throat go slack.

Each bump in the road, each pothole and each curve, the elementary school on Johnson Street, the turn right, the mechanic shop on Douglas Drive, the turn left, Main Street and a streetlight, all the intricacies of direction between her house and the grocery store were obstacles, man-made perversions that stood rigid and motionless, waiting to trip her up with a wrong turn here or a flat tire there. Oredia manipulated the wheel with one hand, her knuckles knotted and white, and pushed at the gearshift with the other, the movements of both arms and legs synchronized, octopus-like, on top of the seat. Hunched in the car with parts of her body jerking against wheel and clutch, brake and gearshift and gas pedal, Oredia felt that a second's lapse of attention, a moment of daydreams or idle wishes, would cause the car to careen into some immovable object, and her body parts would shrivel into the seat like the remains of a swatted spider.

Sometimes the car drove itself, and she watched the wheel turn without the consent of her hands, and the scene through the front window shifted miraculously: the sun behind her, then beside her, then right in front of her, so that her eyes squinted into thin creases. She pulled down the visor, but the sun leapt to the side of the car and rose above the horizon of the door. Trees flickered past the windows, telephone poles and houses raced backwards along the street, ditches and gullies flowed pell-mell and crooked in reverse. In the sky, birds fluttered and dove, their bodies thin pencil marks that suddenly beat crosses and flapped against the blue. And then, up ahead, there was the jeep with him in it, his face a solid grayness as it moved nearer and nearer, beside her, behind her in seconds, and she drove on, watching the world tilt sideways, watching the world slide soundlessly backwards.

Once, Sheba remembered, she had walked onto the far side of the mountain, the Guntown side, where drunk men screamed and played games. She had watched them, her body hidden in the ravine of an old stream. They carried jugs of liquor—"moonshine," the neighborhood kids would whisper, nudging each other—and, howling with laughter, they grouped around an immense oak tree. On the platform a donkey with round, embarrassed eyes stood, imbalanced. The men heaved on the ropes, laughing, while the donkey stumbled stiff-legged across the wood. Sheba had watched until the sun began to drop over the mountain, and then she raced back to her side, heart pounding in her lungs, her mouth gasping like a horse suddenly and sharply reined.

"Go home," she said, still gasping. "You men, you go on home and leave that donkey be." Then shouting, lungs full of air and outrage, "You hear me? You hear me? Get on home, I say leave it alone. You hear me?" A squirrel flickered and flew from branch to branch above her head, a noiseless shadow that leapt into midair, joined suddenly by two, then three more, until the sky was a swath of dipping squirrels. "Go home," she yelled up at the squirrels. "They'll get you, too, they'll laugh at you. Go home, everybody, go home, you hear me?"

"Come back, come back home to me," her father had said, eyes tearing. His mouth clung to the telephone receiver, kissing it. "Please come back." He crouched against the wall of the den, his shoulders hunched around the phone, his whole body quivering, wanting to cram into the phone and writhe across the wires to her mother. Sheba knew it was her mother's voice coming out of the box and into her father's ear. She knew that soon her mother would come home and they would all laugh and shout together, would dance and hug and wring their fingers in excitement. They would play music maybe, and sing out in the kitchen where even the dishes would crash like cymbals. Then she'd tap her feet, listening to the strange click of her patent-leather shoes against the linoleum.

Oredia watched the wheel spin in her hand, the car turning, and she felt her mind throb at the edges, while the road ahead blurred before her eyes. Her whole family, both sides, some crippled from wars, some crippled from age, some sound in mind and body but very fat, all the cousins and aunts and uncles and in-laws gathered in her mind as they had for Sunday dinner. *They sat at picnic tables, women on the left side, men on the right puffing at fat cigars, and children gallivanted through the clearing, laughing and shouting, tripping over roots and picking themselves up. Oredia sat on a stump and watched them. Someone built a fire and changed the loose faces into shadowed outlines. Eyes became dark pits, nostrils twin pockmarks, mouths yawning abysses that sputtered and vomited sounds into the darkness. Instead of warmth Oredia felt the fire give off confusion, a kaleidoscope of belches and tobacco smoke and fragmented conversation.*

"The whole idea," one voice said, jumping out from a picnic table, "the whole idea is to marry them off quick, then let him try and keep her at home. It's the only way, else they parade up and down in public and make a laughingstock of a decent family. Let him do it—can't tie them to their bedroom doors when they're grown."

There was silence for a while, wood popped and burned, and Oredia eased her bottom off the stump and settled it on the ground. Pine needles cracked and poked up below her until she squirmed a niche among them. And then the voices flowed on, stabbing out and up like the ebb and flow of the firelight.

"Married one of those Cherokees from out in the Smokies, raised a whole kit of yellow kids, then came running back to me when her husband took a shotgun and blew all the windows out of their house."

"Should've just shot her and put her out of her misery."

"Should've shot himself and her."

"Kids, too, none of them worth a hang, either."

"So I crept up real quiet-like, damn near lost a knee on some broken glass, and there they were. Kissing and hugging and carrying on in back of the church. I like to've died."

"Take your fist like so, put the bolt in the crook of your knuckles, and then you could take the chin right off of any man. Aim a little lower and you could break his neck—snap—and barely skin your fist."

"Big as a goddamn jackass, never seen a deer so big, aimed below the

head and brought her home in back of the haybaler. Could've stuffed her
head for my den if my kids hadn't run off with it."

"And so I get paid not to grow cotton, just to sit around cleaning my
nails with my teeth."

"Sheba!"

Her father stood by the telephone, staring at her, a look of
amazement on his face, as if he just that minute recognized her
to be someone he'd known for a long time. Dangling horribly
along the wall, the telephone looked like some broken-necked
rat with a mutilated, corkscrewed tail. One time her father had
found a rat in the basement and he screamed, beating it sense-
less with a broom.

"Sheba, oh Sheba, we're saved! She's coming home," he shouted,
looking not at her but at the telephone, then his arms were around
her and she was drowning in his shoulder, breath convulsing in
her throat. He was choking her.

"Daddy, quit it," she tried to say, though the words trapped in
her neck so that she pushed at him, pushed him away and
scrambled to her feet, taking great gulps of air. Her father hung
over the easy chair, arms grabbing at nothing now, his mouth
telling the emptiness: "She's coming back to me, coming home."

Her mother came back on a hot afternoon much later, years
later, Sheba thought, and her mother and father met in the living room, neither of them smiling, although her father pecked
and plucked at her mother who stood stiffly, unmoving, while
he fussed around her.

"We'll never discuss this, never," her mother said. "I've come
back on the condition that we never discuss this."

"Never. I love you, I love you."

He kept bowing his head and mincing back and forth in front
of her; Sheba imagined her mother throwing a stick into the
front yard and her father chasing outside after it. But the next
day, and for days and days after that, they would fight and tussle
and say loud words.

"Did he touch you?" her father demanded, arms crossed upon
his chest, his nose a flat beak with flared nostrils. "How many
times did he touch you?"

"I won't discuss this."

"Twice? More than twice. Say three, maybe six times? Dear God, was it more than that?"

"Shut up, Harold, just shut up. Sheba will hear you."

Sheba sat on her bedroom floor, peeped through a crack in her door, and listened very hard. When they were quiet, she heard the steady throb of her own heart and she tapped her finger to its cadence.

"Did you think of me at all? Did you think of me when he touched you? Tell me—tell me how many times. It's my right, Jesus Christ, it's my right to know. How many times?"

"Yes, damn you, yes. He touched me, I touched him. Enough. I've had enough."

"You *what*?"

There was quiet again until her mother ran wild-eyed into Sheba's bedroom and maneuvered Sheba in front of her. Sheba just stared as her father high-stepped toward her room with a thick mirror in his hands. His face was not her father's, was no one's. It looked like the blankness of a single fingertip.

"I'll kill you! I should kill you."

"The child, Harold! Sheba, Sheba."

He fell, abruptly, onto the floor and started to cry, a big heap of leg and arm and backbone. The mirror shattered against the open door; shards of glass fell in front of Sheba, and her father's neck, her mother's hip, her own face all reflected like patchwork in the pieces. Sheba wanted to put the mirror back together again, to make a photograph that would freeze the fragments of her family into a tight, everlasting whole. They would hang it in the living room over the rust-colored couch; they would love each other very much in the picture.

"How much?" Oredia asked, looking at the outstretched palm of the cashier and below that the brightly colored quart of milk, the lumpy egg carton, a winking cookie man, butter and sugar and tea.

"Five forty-three," the palm demanded, and Oredia paid the money, picking up her own bag and leaving the store. Outside, she walked directly to her car, set the groceries on the front seat, and settled in beside them. Across the parking lot scores of cars were parked in geometric designs along the pavement. They formed a sea where people treaded and craned their necks, nervously looking for their vehicles, bobbing among fenders and tires and reflected sunlight, as if the very asphalt might rend asunder and swallow them before they found their cars. An old woman dressed in black and crowned by a black felt hat with feathers paced up and down between parking spaces. The woman's fingers rustled like branches against her face, her eyes twitched here and there, wrinkles puckered and stretched in agitation. She was lost, adrift at sea. At last Oredia climbed out of her car and approached the woman.

"Can't you find it?" she said, hiccupping the words, as if she, too, were bewildered.

"It was right here, I know it was, right here, and now it's gone." Wildly, the woman twisted her neck toward Oredia, the feathers writhing against the felt of the hat. "I've got to get home and somebody's stole my car. Right here, I say, and now it's gone." She flapped her arms and pointed her fingers, her feathers ruffling up and lilting in the wind. She blinked her eyes. She touched her cheek. Then she turned quickly around and walked briskly toward the grocery store. Oredia got back in her car and drove away.

Through her window Sheba watched her mother's car pull into the driveway, followed closely behind by her father's truck. Then the back door slammed and her mother called "Sheba!" through the rooms. She stood up, holding tightly to her crayon, and walked into the kitchen.

"He's here, but don't worry. It'll be all right. You just sit at the table and don't worry."

Sheba noticed that her mother's hands shook, as though they wanted to flutter away into the air, into the sky. A pink and green gingerbread man blinked up at her from the kitchen table. Standing on the porch, her father knocked at the screen door and pressed his nose flat against the mesh. the knuckles of his fingers like bald mountains as he struck the metal. Her mother opened the door.

"What do you want now?" she asked.

"I've come to give Sheba her allowance," he said, not looking up from the floor, just standing in the square pocket of air made by the open door.

"Then give it to her."

Her mother stood aside while he lumbered across the threshold, hands plunged deep in his trouser pockets. He sidled over to Sheba and loomed above her, his jaw slack upon his collarbone. With one hand he searched a pocket for change, brought out a set of keys and a nickel; then he pulled his wallet from a back pocket. Inside were a five- and a ten-dollar bill. He screwed his face into a fist and held the five in front of Sheba.

"It's just fifty cents, Daddy. I only get fifty cents."

"Take it," he said, almost leaping, legs bent and quivering, and she took it.

"Now you can leave," her mother said, holding on to her hands.

"This is my house!" he roared. Unmoving, he seemed to fly in every direction. The kitchen grew small, though Sheba felt she wasn't there, was somewhere else, and pretty soon she would come back and there would be a pretty gingerbread man to eat.

"Get out, Harold. Please leave, please. I can't deal with you anymore."

"This is mine. You—you bitch! You bitch! I'll kill you," and his hands were around her throat and she screamed: "Call the police, the police, Sheba!"

Sheba ran. She ran outside, across the driveway, blood so thick behind her eyes that she stumbled, jumped up, ran to Mr. Miner's house. Gagging, she told him to call the police—"He's killing her! He's killing her!"—and soon the red lights, flashing, hiccupping, were outside their house. But her mother stood at the front door with two big men who wrote scribbles into thin black books. People from the neighborhood gathered in bunches across the street, whispered, pointed, and shook their heads. They looked like flies, their skinny arms rubbing together, their wide eyes staring, staring. Sheba wanted to swat them with her hand and watch them scatter away. Go home, she would tell them.

That night she lay in bed for a long while. She heard her mother sob in her bedroom, maybe because she didn't die, or maybe because she would. Sheba didn't know. At last there was no sound in the house, but she heard a hundred voices, all of them indistinct, blurred together, a whole crowd of empty voices.

They had nothing to say and, finally, they died, leaving her in silence. Through her window, shafts of moonlight darted onto the floor in swaths of yellow. The church chimes beat out the time—twelve o'clock. Sheba knew that everyone was asleep, her mother and her father, Mr. Miner and that man, the squirrels and the snakes, everyone was asleep. The whole world slept now, but she was awake, looking at the thick moonlight. She started to cry because she was awake in the night, alone and awake while all the people in the world slept. She was afraid she might see something.

The Professors

I have yet to understand it.

When that lavender letter with a foreign postmark arrived from Mrs. Edna Leikin, née Freiman, the woman had been eight years a stranger. "I am free at last!" she wrote. "I grasp now! what an education in passion means." I do not doubt Mrs. Leikin's grasp, nor do I doubt her freedom, but as I said: I have yet to understand it. If a person is lost to you for eight years in a country such as ours, that person quickly becomes an unknown. Mrs. Leikin was not always a stranger.

For nearly two weeks, the first two in June of 1973, I was a guest in her home. Having just graduated from a small university in the rural Berkshires of Massachusetts I wanted nothing more than a vacation of quiet time to compose myself. Somewhere I'd gotten the idea that this was what recent graduates with a bent toward the individualistic were supposed to do. In truth I was uneasy, confused, broke, unfit for any mainstream occupation; I felt I was an educated idiot; but it seemed to me at the time that two weeks would more than prepare me for whatever unique mark I might soon make in the world. My view of freedom was beyond the romantic. I believed that had I gone into any large bookstore, picked out a novel, and brought it to the clerk, shouting "I am too poor to buy this book, but I am an American," I fully believed the man would have given me the book, and perhaps two more besides. Armed with all of these convictions, and convinced I was above the perceptions of my peers, I moved my books and a trunk of clothes into Ms. Freiman's house. She was not then Mrs. Leikin.

We had met before under unusual circumstances. One evening, in the winter of my last year, I was caught outside when one of the tremendous blizzards that regularly rove the area hit with such force I had to run for cover. The nearest shelter was an imposing Gothic building known as the Other Language House. It rested on the site of a previous language building which had been razed in 1853, but the adjective *other* still remained long after those to whom it made a difference were dead; it was often attributed to a Mr. Morris Other, a member in good standing of B'nai B'rith. I ran for it there.

Once inside I became horribly depressed: nearly two dozen faculty and students warmly conversed, wine in hand, while two great fires roared from open grates on either side of the room. I say "depressed" because during that year my moods, particularly the bad ones, had taken on the peculiar aspect of a constantly flipped coin. Any thumbnail could trigger a bottomless despair. A solace in those times was often the recollection of a budding artistic temperament I felt to be welling like a second skin just beneath the surface of those moods. My concepts of freedom and the artist were very much alike. In this case the depression was not triggered by the cozy academic scene I'd happened upon. I had carried the mood inside with me and only named it while standing there in the entranceway of the Other Language House. I cursed the blizzard for setting the temper of the evening, I cursed the people around me for looking happy. The real reason I cursed at all was, I'm afraid, that my boyfriend Sterling P. Kinsale had just gotten a poem published by what we called at the time a "major publication." The ostensible rub inflaming my sensibility was that I had typed it and corrected a misspelling before he sent it off.

I stood on the threshold of all the gaiety and stared wretchedly, wished them all dead, hallucinated a vision whereby everyone present chatted just as gaily in the blizzard outside, their wine frozen over, their breath fogging and mingling. I have noticed since that the capability for mental cruelty in college students closely resembles that of certain divorced peoples and moral groups. For quite a while I stared with a vengeance at plaid trousers, pink sweaters, and down vests until at last I focused in on one pale old man. He stood by the nearer of the fires, his hands behind his back as if straitjacketed there, his eyes fixed hypnotically on the fire opposite him. At first glance he looked like a faculty child so tiny was his stature, but on top of his head there sat a bowler hat, and under the hat was an expression of such exquisite misery that I fell in love with him on the spot. It was all I could do to keep from sprinting over to where he stood, miserable, against the flames.

"Mind if I share your fire?" I asked him. This was broached in a slightly hysterical and out-of-breath voice, though the old man in the bowler hat merely stared unhappily across the room. I began to think him hard of hearing. "Hell of a night, isn't it?" I said, tentatively, a little louder.

"My wife died last year and I don't talk much," he said, not moving an inch.

There is a feeling one can get when utterly moved, and I have felt it only four times in my life. Once, when a cohort of mine was beaten unmercifully by a jeweler for a crime I myself had committed, I felt it. Later still I was bequeathed, on my twenty-seventh birthday, a volume of personal poetry by a grandmother I had never known, and I felt it. I felt this then.

"Sir," I said to the old man in the bowler hat who continued to stare ahead, as if he had met his own eyes across the room. "Sir," I said, "please talk to me." He neither spoke nor, I believe, even blinked, but he moved one small step to the side. I received this as a hearty invitation and stepped closer to the fire and to him. We said nothing for several minutes.

"My wife was the best wife a man ever had!" he shouted abruptly. I nearly jumped into the fire. Several plaid faculty pants turned discreetly in our direction, yet the two of us must have given the impression of never having spoken a word in our lives. I was petrified. The old man in the bowler hat seemed not to have expressed an articulate emotion since the day he was born, and all plaid pants quickly resumed their conversations.

"Have to lower your voice," I whispered conspiratorially.

"Where is the men's room?" he asked in the same tone.

"Up a flight of stairs and on the right," I whispered and pantomimed, as though my life depended on it.

"Thank you," the old man said. Unaccountably I felt the need to marry him posthaste so constricted were my feelings, but he teetered directly enough toward the men's room. If he had gone in the wrong direction I believe I would have set out at once through the blizzard for a Justice of the Peace. In a minute, though, he was back again.

"And I'm on the threshold," he shouted into the fire, "of marrying the *second* best wife in the world," then he teetered back toward the men's room.

A few words describing my temperament, as well as that of a certain breed of college seniors, is in order here. We were a generation on the cusp of an undeclared war that had just been called off "honorably" and a presidency that was about to be called off "dishonorably." That is to say, we were slightly imbalanced; somehow a very important weight had jumped off its end of the teeter-totter while we were still in the air. It seemed impossible to react at any length for, or against, anything. All of this is to explain, inadequately, why I was able in a swift mental sleight to believe the man I thought of marrying one minute was really a stark staring lunatic the next. What's more, I liked him equally well as fiancé or maniac: he had style, and style it seemed to me at the time, was for good or bad the only reaction one could then admire. We were an impotent college generation.

For a while I stood by the fire and tried to imitate the old man in the bowler hat, stared at a fixed point across the room, looked morbid, kept my arms rigidly down my sides like metal girders. The position was intensely uncomfortable and must have resembled the facade of a recently condemned building. No one, however, was looking. I labored like this until the old man returned, resuming his place by my side with all the aplomb of a visiting dignitary. The top of his hat came level with the breach of my nose.

"Congratulations," I told him.

"I never said it would be easy," he said.

"No sir, you never did, not to *me* anyway. Not to my knowledge."

"While the cat's away the mice will play!"

"Right," I said.

"Women are all bastards at heart." I kept quiet at this, although I did move imperceptibly toward the door, and entirely abandoned my imitation of the old man in the bowler hat. Things had taken a turn for the worse.

"They'll take every cent you've got"—and here he looked up

into my face for the first time—"then, *then* they'll up and die on you!"

I began to think it was more than time for me to go mingle with the academic set, but at this point our conversation, *his* conversation rather, was interrupted by the approach of a woman who looked, oddly enough, like a very small whirlwind. She was a short, plump, dark-faced woman whose limbs and torso seemed to be in a constant rotation; she looked like the old man's shadow stirred up savagely.

"Daddy!" she shouted. "You're enjoying yourself with the ladies, are you?" The old man continued to peer forward with that grim intensity I was already wise to, and for a moment I thought the woman had addressed me. Her very gaze rotated without direction around our general vicinity.

"Daddy!" she shouted even louder. The two of them couldn't speak without either a shout or an exclamation so that, caught in the middle as it were, one had no height advantage whatsoever.

"A case in point," said the old man. "Goddamn women!"

"Excuse me," I said and sidestepped for the door.

"Wait!" cried the old man.

"Don't move even an inch!" said the whirlwind.

"I have a very important engagement thirty minutes ago," I said, amiably enough, although I had frozen, awkwardly crouched, in my tracks. I felt something like a criminal giantess in a land of living megaphones. To tell the truth, as a college senior I was so much more backward, more inept, more ignorant of social niceties than my peers that I had for four years existed only by copying *their* demeanors in any given situation. On my own I was a friendly and desperate trapped rat. Nevertheless, if interrogated, I would have defended my individuality and my independence like a rabid politician.

"Come here a moment!" demanded the woman. She motioned me over for a private tête-à-tête, and I hastened to oblige her with a facial expression of profound silliness. "I want to thank you," she said, "for entertaining my father."

I told her the pleasure was probably all mine.

"No, no," she said. "Don't be insane! I think I know my own father well enough."

I pointed out that she very likely did, and that I, too, knew him well enough, and perhaps we should keep our voices down.

"I just want you to know how much I appreciate it." She rotated toward the groups of faculty and students socializing around the room. "Not a damn one of *them* bothered to so much as say hello to him." I glanced at the staring old man, then at the happy, eloquent groups, and didn't say a word. Briefly I believed that I was the only crazy person in the room.

"What I want to tell you is this," she said. "I'm a professor of Russian here at the university, and if there's anything, I really mean *anything*, I can ever do for you, let me know and I'll try to do it. My name is Edna Freiman and my address is in the book. I watched you and you were very kind to Daddy and I appreciate it more than you can know."

I thanked her, then I thanked her father, though God knows from sheer embarrassment—he nodded curtly—and then I left the Other Language House and went home under the withering blizzard. This, then, was my introduction to Ms. Edna Freiman.

I doubt I will see Mrs. Leikin, née Freiman, again, nor do I believe I will hear from her. There was no return address on her letter—posted somewhere in Italy—and the writing itself had all the earmarks of one of her spontaneous exclamations of passion that invites no considered response. Her shouts drifted to me across an ocean, only to recede back into the murmurings of vast and teeming continents. Had her grasp of freedom and her education in passion come from the Soviet Union, or Israel, or Antarctica, my private response would be the same: I have yet to understand it. I did not understand it those two weeks of early summer in 1973 and I don't believe I will ever, even given several lifetimes, understand. If truth is really an ever-increasing complexity, like an evolving tapestry rug, or like a hypnotist's pinwheel, then through Mrs. Edna Leikin I found at the inexperienced age of twenty-one my first real study in mortal truth.

My last semester at the university ticked away uneventfully enough, as, upon recollection, all college semesters seem to go. I passed it, like my peers, in a state of suspended disbelief, all of us having experienced for three and a half years the various unrealities of "getting educated." Or, to put it bluntly, all of us having lived a fifth of our lives in pursuit of leaving, nobly and

entirely, the whole shebang behind us. I have mentioned before
that we were a decidedly causeless generation of students. However, upon graduation, a vicious kind of paralysis set in. It was
as if, since we were no longer suspended in disbelief, we were
rendered cataleptic by our plunge into what we'd never really
tried to believe. We were utterly—doomed to be, it seemed then—
free. Free to fail, free to overcome, free to suffer indignities.
Free to become honest or downtrodden or splendid or crazed.
Free, in essence, to be the ugliest possibility within our imagi-
nations, or conversely, the most impossibly magnificent. At this
point I made an exploratory foray into rain-checked, or rather,
blizzard-checked good graces, and telephoned Ms. Freiman.

She'd be delighted! she cried. With two women such as we in
one house, nothing could stop us! I reserved comment, but
thanked her profusely. She told me to call her Edna. I said I
would. She asked what day she should expect me. I said in about
three hours. She was delighted! and would leave the door unlocked. I thanked her again, then hung up the phone.

For some reason, during the conversation I broke into a hor-
rendous cold sweat and my hands shook, so much so that I nearly
beat myself stupid with the telephone receiver while chatting
with Ms. Freiman. I took this to be an omen. Almost every incident surrounding my graduation had had a tinge of the ominous—a certain gleam in the president's eye when he handed
me the diploma, a bizarre metallic taste to the celebratory glass
of wine, a cloud the shape of an Indian tipi that floated sedately
over the podium. All my wits and energy had for two days gone
into the suppression of rising panic and reckless superstition. I
grinned indiscriminately at passersby. I alternately wept and
guffawed when accosted. I hooted with laughter on parting with
Sterling P. Kinsale, who had joined the Peace Corps. I cried for
an hour over a quarter I'd lost down the grate of a sewer.

I thanked God my parents weren't there to share this joy. They
lived in East Tennessee. They still do, as has every other relative
born in the United States after our forefather settled there from
Ireland, searching for riches in 1793. He didn't find them, and
neither did anyone else in my family. My parents, though,
had splurged and sent a telegram that read WE HOPE YOU'RE

HAPPY STOP—a message, bless their hearts, I find ambiguous even now.

My apartment that year overlooked the main street of a tiny township that the university had subsumed as though it were another fraternal order. I calmed myself by staring maniacally out the window at a drugstore awning across the street. The alternate green and white stripes soothed my spirits; I imagined lying on it hammock-style with an iced ginger beer. Only when the owner rolled it up, signaling a blatant end to the working day, did I get down to the business at hand. Everything I owned was packed in a trunk and a box, and my apartment had the barren, forlorn look of a child's picture of a room. It had no *there* anymore, just straight lines and obscure smudges. My poems, for of course I fancied myself a poet, were in my back pocket. I was ready to go, so I left, oppressed by the many omens one can find in empty rooms. Had Ms. Freiman reneged on her generosity I would have sat for two weeks in that apartment, picking many more omens from thin air.

With the aid of a borrowed handcart I trundled my books and clothes the half mile to my vacation home on the outskirts of university property. That particular afternoon was lovely, and with each laborious tug on the handcart my spirits grew. This, it seemed to me, was the beginning of my real-life mature experience. Around me the campus that for so long had been home took on an inviting foreign aspect. The motley-shaped buildings, shrouded by lush blue-green trees, might have contained dadaists in windowless French rooms or women in chadors, praying to the Most Merciful and Compassionate. Over my head the same sky that had covered all humanity from the first birth to the last, covered me. Tugging and gasping and sweating, I enjoyed my freedom like a child then.

In time I reached the home of my patroness. It was a white two-story clapboard house, built in the usual New England style and surrounded by squat evergreen shrubs. One of the dormer windows caught my eye and immediately I knew that it was mine, that it would make the perfect artist's studio, and that I would write brilliant poetry looking out of it. Full of myself and the world at large I negotiated the handcart onto Ms. Freiman's front porch, opened the door, then backed into the house, handcart in tow. This is what I saw: the woman, whom I remembered as a miniature whirlwind, crouched underneath a Victorian dining table sobbing and moaning as if her heart had been severed. Little bits of yellow notepad lodged in her hair, on her clothing, along her arms; a telephone had been ripped from the wall and lay in the middle of the floor. What terrified me at the time were the little pieces of notepad. Ms. Freiman had changed from a small whirlwind to an even smaller dust devil in the six months since I'd seen her, and my first thought was that, if an ant could lift ten times its weight in dead beetles, then Ms. Freiman was now a force of inconceivable potential. I thought the notepad pieces stuck to her from sheer vacuum.

"Who are *you*!" she cried, her eyes puffed and slightly askew. Once again I mistook the target of her regard, thought perhaps she addressed some interested bystander who had just dropped in for a glimpse of the action. I looked over my shoulder at no one. "What are *you* doing in *my* house?" I concocted a desperate lie concerning wrong addresses and moving companies, but Ms. Freiman was crawling headfirst out from under her dining table.

"Of course," she said and stood up. "You're that kid who's staying here." Nonchalantly, a little sullenly to my mind, she moved over to a coffee table and lit a cigarette, studying me with an unfocused gaze. "Well," said she, "of course you'll have to excuse the state of things."

"O, of course," I repeated like an automaton. And then, not knowing what the hell to make of her, or the situation, or myself for that matter, I said, "Which things?" and smiled madly in her direction.

"Are you blind or what! Everything, sweetheart, every goddamn thing."

"Right," I said. "Everything."

"In fact," she said, exhaling smoke, "my earthly happiness just ended because *that*"—she pointed vigorously toward the sad old phone sprawled on the floor—"that *machine* disconnected my husband-to-be from me forever. Forever, I tell you." Ms. Freiman broke down into sobs again, while still puffing expertly on her cigarette, and I wanted to laugh immoderately, or else join her in brokenhearted tears. Instead I indicated my sympathy

with a fatuous smile and stood at parade rest beside my handcart.

"For heaven's sake!" she shouted, "sit down. You make me
nervous as a cat."

I promptly sat down on the floor.

"Not *there*, you nitwit, sit in a chair."

I jumped to my feet and jogged the three feet to the nearest
chair, an easy chair that had seen better days, situated underneath a full-length mirror. Two of me, it seemed, were perched
like parakeets on the chair cushions. Ms. Freiman moved to a
davenport, sat down, then began to pick the pieces of notepad
off her arms and face with her free hand.

"Do you know anything at all about passion?" she asked me,
indifferently.

I thought she said "fascism," and was about to remark that as
a matter of fact I thought I knew a thing or two after only five
minutes. But Ms. Freiman was the quicker of us.

"Passion," she said, "is what would be left over if every other
human quality were to fly into an abyss." I nodded encourage-
ment, if only to intimate that, although I may well have been a
nitwit, I was nevertheless a good student, but that was Ms. Freiman's definition, in its entirety, of passion. She impressed me
immensely.

A word or two is needed here to distill the situation accurately.
At the time I was essentially homeless, friendless, flat broke, and
naive enough to believe that all those qualities were somehow
romantic. My personal definition of passion was an incredibly
vivid picture of my father at twenty-nine, teaching me lay-ups
with a basketball the size of my entire upper body, shouting across
the court in no uncertain terms—"Bounce it with your heart,
damnit, *with your heart!*" Interspersed with that picture were
various other shots: my mother with a bottle of cod-liver oil in
one hand and a lollipop in the other, the profile of Martin Luther
King, a short story by Flannery O'Connor, the stump of an oak
tree struck by lightning. My definition, then, was a mosaic of
subjectivity, so far from being nameable in one coherent sentence that Ms. Freiman seemed both astute and self-confident,
what I thought a mature woman of experience should be. I was
accustomed to the long-winded approach to conversation of col-

lege students and, in my romanticism, believed that this un-equivocal declarative sentence was quite possibly the one true definition of passion. My artistic motto during this period was to hit the nail repeatedly on the head, to beat it to death, in effect, before it got away. My poetry was rather like a series of concise, scarcely veiled threats directed toward the unparticular. Ms. Freiman embodied the kind of style my instinct had led me to believe was infinitely, even rabidly, attractive.

"I'm an *overly* passionate woman really," said Ms. Freiman. "The least damn little thing can break my heart."

"I'm sorry to hear it," I said.

"Sorry!" she cried. "It's the single saving grace of my personality. You don't understand. I'm an intellectual product of the sixties; I'm not like you kids today with your corporate this and your management that."

I pointed out that I was neither a this nor a that, that I was, in fact, a poet, and wasn't averse to saying so then and there.

"O my God!" she shouted. "Another one of *those*." She began to cry again, not the heaving sobs but a petite, pretty sort of weeping. She could have been a modern Little Nell, a Victorian kind of emotional product of the sixties, except that she was burning her davenport with a cigarette butt.

"Excuse me," I mentioned in a conversational tone, "but you're burning your couch."

"I'm sure I am," sighed Ms. Freiman sadly. "Listen, if you're staying here for two weeks, you better know the whole story."

"You might as well put that cigarette out."

She did so, absentmindedly, and continued. A hole the size of a walnut had already eaten into the upholstery.

"I am engaged to a writer in Moscow, an excellent and *brilliant* poet." Her emphasis on "brilliant" left no doubt in my mind concerning where I stood, with my brave and puny proclamation, in her hierarchy of poetry. Somewhere, I should think, in the left field bleachers. "He's been working for an exit visa for eighteen months, eighteen *shitty* months, and every attempt has gone for naught. Six times he's tried and this last attempt—O! it was so promising—this last attempt failed as miserably as all the others. That *machine* gave me the news only twenty minutes ago, and I wrung its neck for the favor." I glanced at the telephone, lying there like a flayed rat, and felt a cold chill at the base of my spine; this was no ordinary professor of Russian. "The difficulty of his leaving," she went on, "is a bitter testimony to his brilliance as an underground poet, but our combined passion for each other, our passion I say, will one day secure *his* freedom and *my* happiness. I have faith, you see."

Here Ms. Freiman took a much needed breather. The plot had thickened, so to speak, to the point that I could hardly inhale through it. Had I been hooked into the room with an iron lung my engrossment with the situation could not have been greater. Here was a setting for international intrigue, men in dark overcoats leaping over electrified fences; women, faithful women—even better, faithful *pregnant* women—needlepointing messages into innocuous pillows; heartbreak, passion, reunions on a grand scale! And I sat not six feet away from the heroine of the piece.

What never once forcibly struck me, however, was that there was a man trapped somewhere in the world someplace he didn't want to be.

"There's more," said Ms. Freiman. She had left the davenport, was picking up pieces of notepad underneath the dining table. Obscured by the table her voice seemed to emanate from the davenport, and I looked toward it in lieu of Ms. Freiman. "I have two more guests coming in five days. Harriet and Sasha. They just arrived from Moscow and need a place, as Harriet says, 'to discuss things,' though God only knows they're both supreme fools and never discussed anything in their lives. *He* can leave Russia on a whim, my Mikhail can't get out with a hundred bribes." She began to whimper under the table.

"But how," I asked the davenport, "can he get out so easily?" In my mind I was typing and filing away every crumb of data, and I very nearly asked for copyrights right then.

"Because he's mad, insane, out of his mind!" she shouted. "A de*fect*ive Soviet can defect without blinking an eye. They *want* him out. A genius they imprison like a dimwitted con man. And the hell of it is, the supremely funny irony is, *he wants to go back*! He's a madman and a fool and Harriet is a bigger fool for marrying him to begin with. Thank God she refuses to go back with him."

I couldn't believe my good luck. An epic poem with parallel structure had dropped into my lap. Two Soviet men, two American women. One couple free and tortured, the other tortured by separation. What it needed was children, a few beleaguered but essentially endearing kids torn between two doting parents.

"Any children?" I asked with the tone of a hardened detective.

"Of course not," she said, "Don't be fantastic! That's how I *met* Harriet. We were students in Leningrad and she got pregnant by Sasha and wanted an abortion. I helped her under harrowing circumstances, you can't imagine. They were fighting even then. They got married and started beating each other up. *Now* they want to come here and dis*cuss* things. All hell's going to break loose in my own home while that sonofabitching fool demands to return to where my Mikhail can never leave."

Mrs. Freiman stood up and deposited the bits of notepad into a wicker basket beside the davenport. Slowly but inevitably she was beginning to shift into the rotation patterns I remembered so well.

"Well," she said, "I suppose I could show you your room."

I told her I would like nothing more. For at the time I wanted above all things to sit down, alone, and re-create the bare bones of a master artwork in progress.

I never did become a poet. It is almost unmentionable what I have become—suffice it to say that, although I wear spectacles on my nose, there is very little autumn in my heart; cool breezes do sweep through, but I have learned to combat them. And I do not reside in the Berkshires of Massachusetts. Nevertheless there are many places in a country such as ours which, though separate, are similar, and geographies tend to tumble around each other through one's mind after a while. I have never practiced the international mobility of Mrs. Edna Leikin, and yet I could imagine it. In my movement from place to place in one country I have found that the changes within myself in each geography often occur infinitesimally, or perhaps not at all. The setting of a change has little bearing on the movement of emotion, on the tides of recognition or the sweep of cool breezes. Picture a scientist's mortar and consider that without the pestle to grind the grains there is no experiment. If you then picture a professor of anything with spectacles on the nose, consider that without the sharp thrust of emotional possibilities to hone the particular understanding there is nothing to teach. Furthermore, there is no one place in a country such as ours where this can be learned, and consequently I have an abhorrence of lecterns in any shape and podiums of any kind. Although I do not completely understand and never will, Mrs. Edna Leikin was my first inkling into the disassociation of place and emotion.

The five days following my initiation into Ms. Freiman's lifestyle I spent furtively writing notes and envisioning handsome hardcover books with my name on the bindings. I was, of course, given the room with the dormer window, a small but terribly quaint room that sent me into ecstasies whenever I sat in it. Most of my time I sat and paid prolonged attention to my own happiness, scribbling when my thoughts turned toward career vistas. Ms. Freiman's bedroom was down the hall and the two guests— in my terms, the other fateful half of protagonists—would stay in the bedroom across the hall from me. Sometimes I heard Ms. Freiman wail out from obscure parts of the house, an "O Mikhail!" from the kitchen or a "Damned irony!" from the bathroom, but for the most part she treated me as well as an uninvited and naive opportunist deserved. In fact we grew rather close during this interim. She had a cornucopia of passion to indulge and I had a real need to hear it. She shouted and wept, I listened and took note. She cursed the fates loudly and I silently blessed them. We could not have been more complementary if a geometrician had drawn us together.

On the sixth day of my internship in passion the guests arrived. Ms. Freiman was out, for she was translating some *samizdat* stories and used the library. Her own home, she said, took on the feel of an underground dungeon when used for the Russian language. I lay on the living room davenport with a dog-eared copy of *National Geographic*, my feet resting on an armrest and a beer on the floor beside me; it had taken me less than two days to shift gears and make myself at home in Ms. Freiman's house. I was idling in neutral when the taxi pulled up.

The first sounds to waft through the screens into the house were those of a thick and low-pitched Russian accent as it bellowed, "More? He wants more? He cannot *have* the more!" This was closely followed by the loud and independent cry of a Brooklyn cab driver: "Buddy, I been listening to you for five hours and there ain't nothing you got that I'd take." Throughout the exchange a bird-like woman's voice, bred somewhere roughly in the Midwest, was screaming "Tip him! tip him! tip him!" in a manner that suggested the problem would be solved if somebody would just listen. Her suggestion, however, was not taken. The voices grew into a crescendo, climaxed by the thuds of two large objects thrown from a medium height, then a door slammed shut and the taxi squealed away.

"You *tip* people to show your appreciation for services rendered," said the midwestern voice.

"What is '*tip*'?" the Russian accent cried. "Gifts to strangers! Harriet, your country is not any sense to it."

"It's a damn graciousness is what *tip*ping is. You don't know anything about *grace*, you lumbering copeck-pincher."

At this point there came a stream of monosyllabic exclamations in the Russian, and then they knocked on the door. I was already there, ear pressed resolutely to the crack, so I opened it. On the porch stood two of the most disheveled, the most anxious, the most cockled people I had ever seen in my life. They were refugees of a higher magnitude, might have had thirty seconds to gather together their prized possessions before the taxi came to take them away. The man was a study in hair, dark brown hair on the scalp and on the face and from the nose and protruding from the pit of the collarbone. He seemed to reverberate with some kind of inner corpulence that expressed itself in random tufts. The woman, whose hair was the color of Iowa corn, was large and farmerettish, an American *muzhik* with intelligent eyes. Both of them looked as though they'd recently participated in a barroom brawl with the drunker faction of combatants.

"*Debchushka!*" the man bellowed upon seeing me and I knew right then, in an instinctive reflex, that this man would level the brunt of his dissatisfaction with all of North America, in general, on my person, that he would be relentless, and that I would affect amusement every step of the way. "Harriet, watch at this, a little child!"

"Sasha," said Harriet. "Get your neck back in your pants and leave her alone."

"Hello," I said and assumed the way of the hopelessly outnumbered. I was busy rewriting certain segments of my epic poem. "Won't you come in," I said.

"The professor's not home?" Harriet asked.

"She'll be here soon," I said, "I'm to make you feel at home."

"Home!" cried Sasha. "What does a child know about the home?"

"I said leave her alone, you jackass," said Harriet. She uttered a few deliberate, under-the-breath Russian sentences and they crossed the threshold with their two cardboard pieces of luggage. As soon as I shut the door they began it, using fluent, even eloquent Anglo-Saxon language. I stood by the door and smiled throughout the exchange.

"I call a child a child," Sasha proclaimed, staring rather blatantly in my direction. "She does not know what the home means."

"Neither do you, you bastard!" Harriet screamed and flung her suitcase on the carpet. "Your home is a fifth of vodka in a rotten, filthy apartment in a rotten, filthy town." And then, as if to nail the point down, she said, "Rotten, filthy, rotten!" at the top of her lungs.

"I know the home. The home is *Russia*." Sasha rolled the "R" very nicely; I began to acclimate myself like a zealous theatergoer. My protagonists' faces were the color of overripe apples. "You smile at us *debchushka?*" he said. "You think something funny happens here? You are a foolish little child, you know nothing of the world."

"And what Sasha, may I please ask, do *you* know about the world?"

"I know where the home lays. It is where I, and you my wife, belong. You are no wife, Harriet, you are an appended conscience!" Old Sasha seemed pleased as punch with his turn of phrase, and I noticed he took a lengthy sidelong glance at the mirror over the easy chair. Harriet stood in the position of a boxer waiting for the fifth-round bell—relaxed and deadly. I smiled ferociously upon them from the door.

"I will not go back there again in my life," Harriet said quietly.

"Then you have no husband."

"I haven't got one now," she said, quietly quiet.

Fortunately, the explosion that hovered over the lip of the next few possible sentences was diffused by the sudden entrance of Ms. Freiman. She burst into the room and caught me on the shin with the door, whereupon I limped, still smiling, a discreet distance farther along the living room wall.

"Edna!"

"Harriet!"

"Edna!"

"Sasha!"

The three of them joined in one big hug, then broke up into smaller, more vehement one-on-one hugs. Everyone looked wonderful, they cried, everyone was glad to see everyone else, what a joyous occasion, someone had lost weight, someone had grown two inches, someone else looked mean as ever. For reasons I understood only later, there was a mysterious, tacit agreement among them, and they spoke English in most cases, although in the English no holds, so to speak, were barred. A notable exception to this rule was Sasha who, whenever compelled to comment on the American lifestyle—in other words, me—would speak in rapid Russian and wait full of suppressed glee for Ms. Freiman's translation. He started in almost immediately, *debchushka* being my cue word, and all three burst into hilarious laughter, as if sharing a particularly apt joke.

"She's a university student," said Ms. Freiman, choking back a stray chuckle. "She's a *poet!*" This struck them as another knee-slapper, so they hooted for several more minutes while I smiled and nodded and waited to be let in on the witticism. At last Ms. Freiman pulled herself together and turned to me. "He said, ha!, he said that the little girl is like the Leningrad whores: she smiles and bobs her head but doesn't know to whom she engages herself. If she isn't careful, she'll pick up that which will eat her heart."

I thought the humor of this was utterly lost in translation. But, as I have said, on my own devices in social situations I was a friendly, desperate trapped rat. Then, too, I had nowhere else to go and no one else to be with. I stood my ground and grinned. I believe I may have even offered a brief, guttural snicker.

"Sit down, sit down everyone." Ms. Freiman ushered her arms

and they scurried to their respective seats. Once more I found myself in the easy chair. Sasha sat on my left in a Victorian love-seat, Harriet and Ms. Freiman on the davenport. As soon as she sat down Harriet leaned over, picked up my beer, and quaffed it, all in one motion, the knob on her throat moving up and down methodically. This pained me more than any joke could possibly have: it was *my* beer and, furthermore, I wanted it.

"Hey there," I said, "that's my beer you're drinking."

"O," said Harriet, "that's all right, sweetheart, we know you're not really a Leningrad whore."

"So little girl," Sasha said, "you are a poet, is that so?" He pretended to regard me with a fixed amusement, but I could tell his gaze skimmed my left ear, went beyond, and hit the mirror right on the money.

"Yes," I said warily, "I write poetry."

"And what have you seen in this world that is worthy of the poet?"

"Come on Sasha," said Ms. Freiman, "she's only twenty-one. Save your crap for the big leagues."

"In my heart I am twenty-one." He put his hand over his heart, approximately three inches below a massive growth of light brown hair. "I ask her what she has *seen*. There are no poets in this country."

"O, I've been around," I said, but no one was listening.

"Edna," said Harriet, crushing my empty beer can between two powerful palms. "Edna, it's been like this for a week. You'd think that every goddamn thing, person, or idea in this country was the product of a perverted kindergarten class. He sees a cop on a corner and says 'Behold!' like as if he'd seen a vision. He sees a can of soda and dances around on the sidewalk like it was packaged arsenic. He acts like a *tip* is some kind of criminal conspiracy."

"*Tip*!" Sasha cried with dramatic disdain.

"Just what the hell is your problem, Sasha?" Ms. Freiman leaned way over, her hands making a circular pattern on the thighs of her jeans. She looked imminently ready for takeoff. "I mean, just what the hell do you think you're doing? You know, of course, that Mikhail failed to get his exit visa for the *sixth* time."

"I am responsible for no other man."

"It's because, because . . . " Harriet was at a loss for words, sputtered a bit, finally hit the words running. " . . . because you are a goddamned ass-backward self-centered son of a *bitch!*"

"Your words are impressive, Harriet. I am unmoved." He shot a wry glance in my direction, regarding himself in the mirror.

"How can you be so selfish, so without *passion?*" Ms. Freiman cried. She seemed to be in the throes of some revolving crisis. "Harriet loves you, you love her, you could be utterly *free* in this country."

"Edna, would you like to hear how I spend my day there? I'd really like to tell you about one day in the life of Harriet. It'll amuse the hell out of you, it'll kill you."

"Stop this!" Sasha cried. "Our lives are not for another's ears."

"This'll kill you, Edna," Harriet went on, "a typical day in my life." She reclined against the davenport as though preparing to recount a nice fairy tale she'd heard long ago. Sasha's features had solidified into the stoniness of ancient concrete. "First I get up at daybreak and fix *his* breakfast before he goes to work. Always, without exception, it's this *por*ridge that tastes like, looks like, *is* excrement. It's the only thing I can find. Then he leaves. For the next nine hours I go into town and hit every shop, black market or otherwise, just to find the next day's meal. Forget about fresh eggs, fresh milk, fresh meat, fresh anything. Everything is either on shortage and nonexistent, or else too dear to buy. Everything we eat you have to add water to." Harriet began to whimper and Ms. Freiman reached over, patted her arm in a maternal way. *Rigor mortis* had set in on Sasha. "He only gives me half the money he makes, half of nothing, and he spends the rest on vodka. Comes home drunk and beats me, or else, if he's *too* drunk, I beat *him*. Then we go to bed and it starts all over again. Tell me Edna, aren't you amused, aren't you just tickled pink with such a life?"

"I'm so sorry, Harriet," said Ms. Freiman, still patting, patting, in my opinion, a little longer than necessary. After all, Ms. Freiman had lived many years in the Soviet Union, too, and it seemed that all the hoopla took on a forced edge.

"I'm so sorry, Harriet," Sasha mimicked in a voice that, surprisingly, resembled Ms. Freiman's. "Sorry! It is of no concern. It is *home*."

At this Harriet jumped from the davenport, bursting outright into tears, and fled from the room, effectively ending discussion. Ms. Freiman followed her, first delivering a curt "Bastard!" over her shoulder, and then only Sasha and I remained in the room. I picked at a string on my shirt, smiled into my own lap.

"So, smiling poet child," said Sasha. "You will write of this then?"

"Maybe," I said offhandedly, as if the subject I had already been writing about for a week were perhaps beneath my dignity.

"Remember then, *debchushka*, you know absolutely nothing." He then stood up, stared into himself via the mirror until, apparently satisfied, he too left the room. I sat alone with my own reflections, revising and shortening certain epic thoughts.

Our party of four reconvened only that night for dinner. Throughout that day voices were raised, doors were slammed, feet marched heavily from room to room, but that night three perfectly vivacious and self-possessed people sat down to supper. Ms. Freiman had gone all out and fixed a tremendous holiday meal. A roast beef the size of a human head, a half dozen vegetable dishes all of which were color-coordinated, two desserts, and two bottles of Soviet vodka, chilled in the freezer. Surrounding the food were Ms. Freiman's best china plates and silverware and delicately blown shot glasses. Sasha slumped manfully at the head of the table, a position that shortly became problematic, at least to me. Before a fork was raised or tidbit sampled, there came a series of interminable, sincere toasts of which Sasha was the sole proprietor.

He toasted the *debchushka* and we drank a shot. He toasted women, then men, and we drank two shots. He toasted a handful of kings, a couple of religious leaders, and several Soviet writers of whom Tolstoi was the only name I recognized. My recognition mechanism was malfunctioning by this time. They all drank shots by the fistful. I began to sip, albeit recklessly, though irritating, frequent giggles kept issuing from my vicinity. As I recall, under my breath I was saying "Hush now, hush" to that giggling fool. When at last Sasha shut up and we were allowed to eat, I could only stare at all the pretty colors that floated ever so slowly around my plate; I believe I ate a pea. The three of them ate with the appetites of lumberjacks, and very little conversation, other than the compliments-to-the-chef kind, took place.

After the meal Ms. Freiman excused herself to run an errand. She left the table in a gray wash, impossibly quickly to my thinking, for during the course of the meal I had been playing an elaborate game that involved chess pieces and the three of them. I was taken aback that someone could move without my direction. This confusion increased by leaps and bounds in the next several minutes, even though I suffered it in a relatively painless state. The first action of consequence was the loud and unexpected crash of a fork against the wall opposite me.

"There's been an *ac*-cident," I shouted abruptly. In fact, I fully believed the room to be tilting on edge, and I even grabbed at my shot glass so as not to see it spilled.

"I refuse to go back there!" Harriet screamed. Another implement, a spoon I believe, went crashing against the far wall.

"But you *will!*" bellowed Sasha. He picked up his fork and threw it toward Harriet's wall. With something like the vigilance of an astronomer I watched the silverware cross my field of vision. They proceeded to throw every single piece of silver within their reach, including the napkin rings, but when they started in on the shot glasses I realized it was high time I went to bed.

"Sit down *debchushka!*" Sasha shouted. "If you are the poet then see the life! Why do you think we speak in your ridiculous language? For you!"

I stayed put, hadn't even known I *had* moved. The room appeared to spin subtly around a fixed point, centered on the remains of the roast beef, and I sat and watched the shot glasses hit the various walls. Everything occurred in a wondrous slow motion, yet I had the presence of mind to save my shot glass. I entertained myself with surreptitious sips amid the shouting and the crashing. A vision of what the retail value of all the thrown objects would be on the black market crossed my mind. At last the brawl took a more physical turn, saving the integrity of the china, and Sasha leapt across the room, grappling Harriet into an awkward half nelson. While they were thus occupied, I made my reeling exit and went to bed.

I slept the big sleep of the rarely drunk that night. Long about 3 A.M., however, I was awakened by what seemed to be a raging party in the bedroom across the hall. In a half stupor I heard delighted yips and squeaks, little ecstatic moans, laughter bordering on hysteria, in short, the sounds of the most active lovemaking I had ever in my life heard. In spite of an enormous act of will, I couldn't keep my eyes open. But even as I dropped off, I knew that the happiness I heard then was, finally, the essence of what kept that miserable couple together.

The days following, five to be exact, were a repetition of the first. Ms. Freiman and Harriet blasted Sasha, entreated Sasha, beseeched and bewailed him during the daylight hours. For his part Sasha gave in not a centimeter. At supper skirmishes took place, although not of the magnitude of the first one, and usually one or another of the combatants resorted to blows. At night the same delicious and rabid lovemaking I had heard while drunk continued on until late in the early morning hours. Sasha maintained his condescending, self-righteous attitude toward my every word, my every silence. I maintained my oblique and simpering smiles. The two women occasionally made halfhearted attempts at my defense, but they were consumed, passionately consumed with the dramatics of the ongoing dilemma. After that first night I stopped writing or thinking about epic poems, hardcover books, or for that matter any brand of artistic structure whatsoever. It was, in my opinion, every *debchushka* for herself, and bedamned with reflection upon it.

Things came to a screeching halt on the twelfth day of my stay at Ms. Freiman's home. It was in the morning of the day before I was to leave—thrust myself, so to speak, into the world—and I had lain rather late in bed. I had certain pragmatic considerations to peruse. For instance, where exactly I would go, what I would do, and how I would get there. The revelry from the night before had extended particularly late, so late that I lost several hours sleep listening intently, but Ms. Freiman was already up and about regardless of noise. I could hear her downstairs rattling dishes. Across the hall the telephone began to ring. Because Ms. Freiman had attacked the downstairs phone, the one in the guest bedroom was the only one left in the house. The telephone rang and rang. After three or four rings I grew increasingly nervous; I expected a call from someone with a tentative ride south, and didn't want to miss it. It was the only concrete deal toward my future I had yet made. I hurriedly put on a robe, stalked the six feet across the hall, and pounded on the door.

"Telephone," I shouted.

"What!" bellowed Sasha.

"Damn telephone," I answered. Through the door I could hear a muffled altercation of sorts, then a flurry of rapidly drawn bedcovers.

"Enter *debchushka*," said Sasha, and I did, just in time to know that the telephone had suddenly, irrevocably, stopped ringing.

Certain details of the ensuing picture are lost in an eight-year blackout. What I did see, point-blank, were two pear-shaped, dark-complexioned breasts that lapped like sea creatures just above the shore of a blanket. On top of one of these creatures rested Sasha's left hand, rather possessively at that. And the mermaid of this Poseidon was, of course, Ms. Edna Freiman.

"Sit down," said Ms. Freiman, patting the space of bed beside her. "Harriet's downstairs making us some coffee."

What I heard instead was a vivid *Passion is what would be left over if every other human quality were to fly into an abyss.*

"You!" I yelled and felt a bottomless, an utter deflation. "You are a goddamned motherfucking piss-ant *hypocrite!*"

I have yet another eight-year memory lapse concerning the next few moments. All I remember is being fully dressed and throwing clothes into my trunk. The material hung over the edge like a falling wave, my box of books sat unopened beside it.

"You don't have to go, you know," Ms. Freiman's voice said from the door behind me. "You could stay all summer if you wanted to."

I didn't answer, but shut and locked my trunk.

"Are we really so terrible?" she asked.

I heaved the trunk and box on top of my handcart.

"Look, you're being incredibly naive, you *must* have heard us all along."

"Excuse me," I said and maneuvered the cart through the door.

"What you believe in with all your heart, and what you do, aren't necessarily the same thing," she said, stepping aside.

I bumped the handcart down each step until I reached the front hall.

"Well, who are *you!*" she cried. "You don't know *anything!*"

I opened the door, pulling the handcart after me into the summer of the Massachusetts Berkshires.

"*You* are the flaming hypocrite!" Ms. Freiman screamed, and I moved resolutely on down the sidewalk.

Ms. Edna Freiman was right, of course. I was. I caught that ride south anyway, ended up in Washington, D.C., with bitter reflections on the fickleness of professed integrity and the hypocrisy of the human heart. But I was wrong. The human heart is an ever-increasing complexity. I did not understand. I never will. Much later, at a dourly wild party in Los Angeles, I came upon a friend of Mrs. Edna Leikin, née Freiman. She had married Mikhail Leikin, then she divorced him within a year, and then traveled throughout Europe hosting a new lover every six months. Her letter to me—posted somewhere in Italy—was a passionate tribute to her latest lover, a Milano with "aquiline qualities." I do not know how she got my address, nor do I care. Suffice it to say that once a person is lost to you for eight years in a country such as ours, that person quickly becomes an unknown.

Mrs. Leikin was not always a stranger.

The Wellest Day

By one in the afternoon most of the family was there. The other son came last and the family watched him through the glass, watched him get out of the car and move toward the house beneath a sky that was evenly gray. It was still an old-fashioned family and so they sat quietly, each in his own way listening to the sounds the house made. Every once in a while Mrs. Smith made a small noise, a hollow, forlorn sound, and then one of the younger women came over to pat her somewhere, on her head, her hand. She was no longer young and they were afraid of what might happen in her mind. By two the rains set in.

"Ray was a good boy," Mrs. Smith said and she seemed to address the rain falling steadily outside the glass.

"Yes'm," one of her daughters answered from the davenport. A little boy came from the back of the house and went to the davenport, pulling his mother's dress with his eyes fixed on Mrs. Smith. "Pull up your britches, please sir," the daughter said, but the little boy was mesmerized; he might have seen something the others couldn't see.

"You think back on the wellest day you ever had," said Mrs. Smith, "and you *still* sick enough to die."

"O Momma!" The daughter hiked up the little boy's pants, then popped him on the behind. He backpedaled to a doorway where he leaned against the doorjamb, still staring, his eyes the color of rushing water.

"More rain like this," the son said, "and there ain't no planting till June."

"July more like it," said the other man, the son-in-law, and he snorted. They both looked through the glass, quiet again.

"Come a day and the rains will wash the earth free of sin." Mrs. Smith sat in a rocking chair, so still only the beating of her heart showed through on her wrists, and she kept looking out the picture window. "Come a day and the sins of man will wash down into the earth and under the earth and on down till . . . "

"O Momma!" said her daughter. Her daughter was a sturdy, unfriendly-looking woman who kept pulling the hem of her skirt over her knees. "Hush now, Momma," she said. "Let's all of us just sit here and be quiet."

Mrs. Smith made a small noise. The other daughter, the one with the kind face, came over to pat her hand, but Mrs. Smith gave a harsh movement and the other daughter sat back down. "It was a day like this, the heat so close it made you crazy, just like this. We used to say, Sarah used to say, 'The devil himself is drowning,' and we all laughed—'That's a good one,' we'd say. Really, just like this." The whole house murmured under the *pit-pat*ting of the rains, and the family, with a sort of general shrug, settled itself down to listen. They had heard the story many times, they had told it themselves many times, and so with the brunt of habit and an old love for their mother they settled down to listen again. Only the little boy against the doorjamb had never heard the story before, but everyone had forgotten him by then. He picked his nose, staring at Mrs. Smith.

"Look out that window and tell me, can you see? I never could, Sarah couldn't neither. They was this idiot boy, Salem was his name, and he could see, could see right through the rain and into the world, into anybody's heart for that matter. 'It's a bad un,' he'd say and just grin, just grin and grin. And first thing you know, there'd come Luke Jacobs or Willie Bean at the door, and they *were* bad uns. Now how did that idiot boy know they was coming? He could *see*, that's how, right through the glass and on into the rain, that boy could *see*. He had eyes the Lord only gives to cripples because they won't be blinded by the emptiness in us all.

"So one day, a day just like this, me and Salem and Sarah were sitting here, like we're sitting here now, and then the rains come. Sarah, she liked Salem and he liked her. The day Sarah died Salem come over here with a bunch of flowers—weeds, they were, dandelions and clover and honeysuckle—and he stood on the

front porch with that bunch in his hands, just grinning and
grinning. I said to him, I says, 'Salem, what you doing way over
here?' but he just grins like I'd said something funny. I says, 'You
come to see Sarah?' and he nods with an almost serious look on
his face. He could be like you or me sometimes. Well, I said,
'Sarah died last night in her bed, don't you know that?' but he
nods and grins and puts that bunch of weeds in my hands. Then
he turns and runs, *runs* I tell you, away from the house. Never
showed up again. That truck on 11-W run him over not two
months later.

"But one time him and Sarah and me were sitting in the house
on a day like this one. It seemed like we all ought to've been
outside building a boat, it was that rainy, and *hot*, Lord the steam
sizzled off the windows. It was a misery. Sarah had her a piece
of paper she fanned herself with, and I remember how the breeze
she made took her hair and made it buck up against the sides of
her face. She was a pretty woman, our Sarah, and you wouldn't
trade the ringlets of hair around her face for any amount of
wisdom. She was *that* pretty. When we were little I used to blame
her for it, but—Sarah—I know where the dust lays now, I don't
place no blame, you had a pretty head a hair. And don't you
know, hair never dies in the grave. Myself, I always could take
the heat, even on the hottest summer day, I could work in the
garden or around the house and still not need the shade. It was
because I sweated, Papaw used to say, like a goddamn pig with
measles. But Papaw always did have a well-oiled mouth, like our
Rebekah, and that man Jenkins shot him because of that, I'm
sure, though Daddy said it was business. Daddy had a simple
mind, bless his heart, and he didn't know the world was chang-
ing. People just as soon shoot you as look at you, you know. Salem
had on his everyday overalls, with the pockets full of odds and
ends. From where I sat I could see a crawdad, an ear of corn,
and a katydid on a string. He always had something unusual
crawling all over him. It was his way. O! the heat was awful that
day and even Salem was jumpy with it. He kept flipping the
katydid away and drawing it back, flipping it away and pulling
back, till I thought I'd have to say something when Sarah says,
'The devil himself is drowning today.' Salem, he takes the katydid and puts it in his pocket. It jumps around through the cloth,

you can tell, but he has a serious look on his face now. Whenever Sarah opened her mouth, Salem got serious, a funny thing when you think of how he was supposed to be an idiot. He was *not* a everyday idiot, is my point, he could *see*, and that's one reason for my telling this."

"Momma," said the daughter with the kind face. "We all got to go in an hour. Can I fix you something to eat?" The rain had shifted in tempo, had fallen into one pure sound, as of a wave cresting steadily across unbroken sea. Even the family had shifted position—the two men leaned on their knees, looking at the floor, the women leaned back against the davenport, looking through the glass. Only the little boy and Mrs. Smith remained where they were, the one against the doorjamb, staring, the other in the rocker with her wrists moving strangely.

"I never could see and neither could Sarah. It has to be in the blood, I mean you have to see your own emptiness before you can see it somewheres else. I mean Salem lived in his own emptiness and so he could see. We all of us in this family, from my papaw to your papaw to your daddy that you only know through my stories, we all so full of ourselves we can't see. That's our way."

"O Momma!" said her daughter. "Can't we everybody sit here and be quiet? On this day of all days can't we all just *be quiet?*" She began to cry a little, sturdy, practical tears, tears that didn't ask to be comforted or noticed. The men, quiet, kept looking at the floor.

"We were all sitting here and that rain and that awful heat made the whole room seem like it was right inside your head, not out there where you could name it, but right inside your head where they wasn't no names. I remember thinking that if a cold breeze had come through we'd all have frozen solid right there in our minds. Sarah quits fanning herself and puts the piece of paper in her lap.

"'It's no kind of day to move at all,' she says.

"'It ain't bad,' I say, because I'm the one the heat's not supposed to bother. The truth is, I was suffering, too.

"'It's a bad un,' Salem says and grins. We both, Sarah and me, we cock our heads. Salem never said that unless it really was bad. Right then I could feel it, something gone sour over the house. I'm not saying I can see, I'm saying I can feel it once it's happened. Sarah could, too. The Lord gives us inklings no matter what the blood. We could feel it.

"'It's them kids,' says Salem and I feel a hand on my throat. You all were only babies then, all you could do was make mischief or crawl or say 'Bye-bye' great big and loud. You were over at the Misses Franklins because they'd gotten lonely and older and I didn't see no harm in giving life to lonely people. They both of them always asked to see you and I didn't see no harm. You liked them. They gave you cookies and sweet ice and you sat in their laps and loved them. You don't remember, but when they died, one three months behind the other, they wanted to give you four everything they had. I wouldn't let them—they had kin and you were just babies that filled in their dying for them. I wouldn't let them. But O! I was afraid for you then. I could see that house of theirs all a-flame, them not knowing what to do but die quickly, you too young to know that everything dies. I was *so* afraid. There was this cold thing right at my throat and it didn't let up at all, kept going tighter as those moments went by between Salem saying what he did and me feeling it."

"This is, this is *such* a damned morbid family!" The daughter pulled her hem over her knees, then seemed to come up onto her feet with the motion of that pulling, and began to pace up and back across the room. No one else moved. "Momma, this is no kind of day for that story. This day of all damn days."

"Leave it," said the son-in-law, "leave it lay, Rebekah, and sit back down." Although he spoke in low tones, still his voice had a roughness over it, calloused like his hands, and everyone knew he meant what he said, even though he was a gentle man.

She sat down again, didn't seem to know where to place her feet or where to rest her eyes.

"Something to eat?" the other daughter asked, politely.

"Listen to that rain, would you," said the son. "Didn't know they was that much water in the whole world."

"*I'm* hungry," the little boy said, and then, after a moment, "Where's Uncle Ray?" No one noticed him and he slid his back along the door until he was leaning at an odd, experimental angle. He stayed like that, testing his balance.

"A course, it wasn't you four at all. After a few minutes of quiet, I knew. I knew. It was like a great white light shining in the middle of a burning hot day, the light bigger and bigger till all I knew and all I could think was that I *knew*. Call it what you will, it was the Lord's voice is what it was, speaking that great white light in my mind.

"'I'm so sorry,' Sarah says and she comes over to me, holds me close, so close, and I remember her hair—her pretty, lovely hair—how it held me, too, from the sweat of her face.

"'They coming now,' says Salem.

"'I'm ready,' I say and I was, I was ready. At first I thought I might not be, I thought they was only so much knowing a body could hold, that I might just burn up in the light. But, no, I was ready, ready for that knock at the door, and so was Sarah—her face! O her face! it was full of paths that hadn't been there before, old paths you only have to push something aside to find. She didn't look old so much as hidden all of a sudden.

"'Sarah,' I say, 'Sarah, I love you dearly,' and that was the first and last time I ever told her. I wish. I wish . . . "

"Momma," said the other daughter, "we all got to go in half an hour. Why don't you eat you something before the service?"

"Why are you so goddamned hepped up on *food* today?" the daughter wanted to know, plucking at her hem. She couldn't seem to cover her knees.

"*I* ain't eat since lunch," the little boy said. He was busy rocking back and forth against the doorjamb. "Where's Uncle Ray?" he asked.

"One more word, little sir," the daughter said, "and you'll be taking a nap."

"I could fix some nice cold-meat sandwiches," said the other daughter, wistfully.

"The knock come with the rain, quick, like it was all the same thing, the pounding coming down at the exact time you expected it to." Mrs. Smith had not yet moved. She sat in her rocking chair and watched the rain through the glass and did not move. Only the little boy against the doorjamb, with the sight of children, noticed the twitching of her wrists. "What happened was, Sarah moved away from me and the last thing to leave was this one wet ringlet. It held on for a moment, minutes it seemed, and finally that was gone, too, and I knew it was my duty to answer the door myself, that of all the people alive in the world I was the only person to answer the door. Salem hadn't really done another thing and, don't you know, he didn't have to? All he was was a beginning, the way all beginnings come out of the blue. The Lord works in the awfulest ways He can, He takes the littlest thing and makes it the only thing you can hold on to. So all Salem had to do was be where he was, seeing, and then He had me where He wanted me. We all of us are doomed, you know. Doomed. I answered the door.

"'O, Lizabeth, don't,' Sarah says, but I go ahead.

"It was Clarence Selby, the one that used to work in the Esso station at Rogersville. I knew him, I knew everything at that partic'lar time, I even knew how he'd look before he got there: soaked to the other side of skin, crazy-eyed, his hair stuck to his face like he'd walked out of the ocean, I knew him all right. He was standing on the steps crying, sobbing really, and I ask him, 'Won't you come in?' but all he does is cry, is sob. Then he goes down on his knees, on his knees there in the rain on the steps, sobbing, and he says, 'It's him! O God, I'm so sorry! It's Glenn . . . ' And he puts his face against my knees and then I'm there, too, down there with his head in my lap, telling him 'It's all right, all right, all right,' and I don't know yet what's happened and still I say, 'It's all right, it's all right.'

"'Bring him inside, Lizabeth,' Sarah says somewhere behind me, though I only hear her from a distance. All at once I'm a ways away, so far away, and I don't want to get back, I'm safe at the bottom of something, but I say, 'Clarence,' I say, 'Clarence,' and he doesn't even know his name.

"'The kids,' Salem says, far away.

"'What's happened?' I ask, finally, and what I meant was 'How, how did it happen?' and no, no, what I meant was 'Why?'

"'O, I'm so sorry—it's him, he just laid there . . . ' We were both of us under the rain on the steps so I couldn't see Clarence, couldn't see anything in that dark and that rain, but I could feel him in my lap. His head felt like a handful of water but my hands were on his neck, tight there.

"'Tell me, Clarence,' I say to him, 'tell me and let's be done.'

"'His head, Lizabeth, his head all swoll up.' Clarence looks up and though I can't see him I know. 'He just laid there with his head all swoll up. I'm so sorry, just swoll up to melon size. I didn't know, Lizabeth, I swear before God Amighty I didn't know.'

" 'I know, Clarence,' I tell him, 'I know where to put the blame and it ain't you. Tell me.'

" 'We was doing it as a favor for Willie Bean. I'll kill the son a bitch for you, Lizabeth, I swear I'll do it.'

" 'No,' I say.

"Clarence, he says: 'It was Willie Bean, him and Luke Jacobs both. Willie and Luke always fighting, you know that, Lizabeth, always one pulling something on the other. Willie said the oak tree was on his land and Luke said no, it was on his. I'll kill both sons a bitches, you say so . . . '

" 'No,' I say.

"He says: 'Willie snuck out after dark tonight and cut the tree down. It was just a little oak tree, not worth a damn to nobody, and Willie cuts it down out of meanness. Luke found the tree down and took his shotgun and went to the sheriff, wanted Willie arrested, wanted Willie hung. He, Luke, said he knew it was Willie by the way the tree fell. It was a *little* tree, Lizabeth, O I'm sorry, a little old tree. Willie finds Glenn and me at my house, comes running in with his face all a-fire and says we got to help him hide the tree. Says we owe him one, but we didn't, we didn't owe that bastard nothing. It was the excitement that done it. Of a sudden it seemed like nothing else in the world would be as exciting as hiding that tree, nothing else would do.'

" 'It's all right, Clarence,' I tell him, because he's trembling so, I'm afraid he'll lose his mind before I know everything, everything the way it happened instead of the way it must have happened.

"He hugs himself and says, slower now: 'We went with him, even forgot our slickers and boots, we was *that* excited. You couldn't see three foot in front of your nose and the rain kept slapping your face like fingers and when we got to the tree Willie says, "Over the creek," meaning the Cherokee, and so we heave it, pull and push it with the mud curling up wherever you touched it until we got to the creek and into the creek with me and Willie pulling and him pushing. It was the excitement that done it. I didn't know, Lizabeth, I swear I didn't know and he must've forgot in the excitement because the tree give way on his end and we look back and he's gone, Lizabeth, like *that* he's gone. His face, his face all swoll up and Luke frowning down on him and the sheriff with a horrible look staring down on him and his face . . . '

"It was over then, I knew. Clarence didn't stay no longer. He was so sorry it was killing him to be near me and he left. Never could look me in the face after that, always crossed the street or tied his shoes or turned and went in the other direction after that. Salem and Sarah were standing in the door, waiting, and I stand up in the rain, look back at them, me standing in the rain.

" 'It's a bad un,' Salem says and grins, and I remember that—how Salem grinned and grinned through the rain."

"It's time to go now, Momma," said the other daughter. "We can eat when we get back." She stood up.

"I'm hungry *now*," the little boy said, but his mother was already on her feet and she hiked up his pants, then popped his behind.

"Hush your mouth and get going, please sir," she told him.

"I can fix us all a nice supper," the other daughter said, "a nice supper when we get back."

"No planting till June for sure," said the son, looking through the glass.

"August more like it," the son-in-law said, snorting, and then the men went out the door together.

Mrs. Smith was the last to leave the house. Although the rain had stopped, it was only a temporary grace, for the sky was an immense, even gray. She watched the family, watched them get into the cars, waiting for her, but she stood on the porch for quite a while, listening to the sounds the house made.

By two in the morning the rains set in again. That sound against her house awakened Mrs. Smith, that pure sound of the murmuring rain. For a moment she lay very still, as though in anticipation of voices, but no voices came. She sat up in the bed, pulling a robe around her. "Come a day," she said in a normal tone of voice, "and the rains will wash the earth free of sin." Mrs. Smith was no longer young and what went on in her mind often ended up out loud. "Down and down it will go," she said. The rain was still falling and she sat on the bed in her robe for a long time. At last she shook her head, saying, "Sick enough and never ready," and then she laughed at that out loud.

Each step to the downstairs was familiar to her feet, so all she had to do was take them as they came, as though the steps, the whole house, was a picture she'd drawn inside her mind. In the living room she stopped and looked through the glass. That's all she did: she stared through the glass at the rain. So intently did she stare, she never saw the little boy who had followed her down.

"A good boy," she said, addressing the rain.

"Mamaw," said the little boy, "Mamaw, why was Uncle Ray so white?"

"Into the earth and under the earth and on down."

"*Mamaw*, why was he so *white?*" The little boy went over and pulled on her robe until she looked at him with no surprise at all.

"I never asked them," Mrs. Smith told the little boy. "I'm not lonely and I don't need nobody to fill in my dying for me."

"I seen a snake come out of its skin," the little boy said, slyly. "It was white."

"No cookies," she told him and looked away. "Nor no sweet ice neither."

"I *seen* it," he said. "White like *he* was. I seen that old snake come right out of its skin and I jumped on its head, up and down on its head, and the stuff that come out was white, too. I *seen* it."

"I never could see," said Mrs. Smith "So full of ourselves, can't see." She was staring outside now, through the glass, and even the little boy knew she wasn't with him. He just stood beside her, staring where she stared. The lightning and thunder came then, illuminating them, bouncing off the house.

"*I* ain't scared," said the little boy, but Mrs. Smith was already a ways away, far inside the rain, so far inside it that she couldn't see the lightning or the glass or the rain itself, far enough inside it that her eyes could no longer see to be blind.

"I ain't scared!" the little boy shouted triumphantly, just as a great lightning was suddenly upon them. "*I ain't scared!*"

Country Blues for Melissa

One night, twenty years ago and in the middle of one of the few really blizzard-like storms that pounce on the mountains of East Tennessee, I awoke from a strange dream—about disembodied but kind hearts, oddly enough, throwing bars of music at me—and felt a very cold draft on my face. My breath came out in wizening white gusts. At first glance I thought my parents, in a fit of instruction, had moved me, bed and all, outside the house into the front yard where I was to learn, through experience my mother would explain, not to oversleep on school days; small children and dogs, she'd say, should be shown, not told. At a second, more desperate glance I stared for a full minute, and as if it were the sole orienting point in a universe run amok, at the broken Timex wristwatch on my nightstand. It read, as it always did, a comforting three-thirty. My meteorite rock sat like a sentinel on the dresser, my picture of the Carter Family (Maybelle on guitar, A.P. at the mike) still hung provocatively over the mirror. All was right, though very cold, with my world.

A proprietary inspection, now sitting straight up in the bed, led to an open, an exceedingly open, window of my bedroom and to the bare feet and white pajama-striped calves of my brother, Alvin, who leaned outside on the sill. Except for a wriggling about the toes, there was no movement at the window, although a trickle of snow and cold air moved quite freely into the room. Across the room and through the bath adjoining our bedrooms I noticed that my brother's window was also open, curtains flapping, an inch-thick accumulation of snow lapping over the sill onto the wooden slats of his floor. At the time, precisely three-thirty in the morning on February 15, 1960, my brother was nine, I was eight. And the two of us, according to a certain blood relative, were the consecutive boy then girl amendments to a flamboyant New Year's resolution made public by our mother at a family Christmas dinner in 1950. It's a pack of lies, she'll say when confronted, however.

"What's going on?" I demanded of the hindquarters upon my windowsill. "What is it, people or what?" From his curious posture a sudden, delightful image of two steel guitarists, a banjoist, an autoharpist, and a fiddler had thrust itself into the blizzard outside and begun to play a rousing version of "Let Old Mother Nature Have Her Way" inside my head. The toes on the sill, pink in the shadows, wriggled a vague response.

My brother, at nine, was one of those levelheaded young men who can with impunity disregard a direct question and then, indirectly, answer it in painful detail much later. Once our father took it upon himself to explain Death to Alvin, apparently because he had watched the funeral of a much-beloved grandmother with an impassive, almost bored six-year-old's expression. After a week of what Daddy termed "embarrassingly blank stares," the lessons were reassigned to a more sophisticated period of his child development. Much later though, in the act of rummaging for stray cigars in my mother's sewing basket, Daddy came across a folded 8- by 10-inch piece of notebook paper that purported to be Alvin's last will and testament, signed the day, month, and year of that first funeral. He had bequeathed all seventeen personal possessions, in their motley entirety, to his deceased grandmother.

"It's cold for goodness' sake, Alvin," I told the left foot, the one closest to my bed. Then, hopefully, "I'll bet it ain't half so cold with all these windows shut. What do you think, Alvin, it's *cold* in here, hey?"

No response, not even a wriggle, not that I expected one, and the wind wheezed more snow onto the floor where it lay in latent dunes, white on black. After eight years of studying my brother, of watching him, rather, like a pensive hawk; reading the books he did or having him read them to me (both of us having acquired this skill at the age of four and a half with the agreement we'd quit when someone ordered us to learn it, which they did, and we didn't); wearing the same clothes right down to the J. C.

Penney cowboy boots; eating the same food (exclusive of certain varieties of mixed vegetables, particularly those with yellows and pale greens); and most importantly, falling deeply in love with the same country music heroes and heroines; after years of this concentrated footstep-following, I trusted, with a violent passion, my brother's most eccentric whim. If he walked with a slight stoop like Hank Williams, I did. If he etched scars of mascara onto his face and swaggered into saloons to prove his manhood, I did, too. We had stacks of our parents' 45s and old 78s, taller than we were, and we lovingly played them over and over on a beaten-to-death battery-operated Sears-Roebuck phonograph. We acted out the more dramatic scenes, parting with great sorrow and many tears in the front yard and reuniting, with harrowing joy and many more tears, in the back yard where the phonograph and Hank Locklin squeaked out "Please Help Me I'm Falling" from a strategic point in the grass. On one notable occasion Alvin climbed an oak tree, tied a rope to one of its highest branches, and stopped just short of hanging himself to the tune of "Dang Me."

There were other symptoms of love that presented themselves at peculiar moments. For a while Alvin took to quoting, verbatim and with a look of profound dignity, the words of Hank Williams responding to a reporter's sophomoric question, "What exactly is the *appeal* of country music, Mr. Williams?" " 'It can be explained,' " Alvin would quote, abruptly, at, say, a dinner party given by our parents, " 'It can be explained in just one word: Sincerity. When a hillbilly sings a crazy song,' " he'd go on, " 'he *feels* crazy. When he sings, "I Laid My Mother Away," he *sees* her a-laying right there in the coffin. He sings more sincere than most entertainers because the hillbilly was raised rougher than most entertainers.' " Here Alvin began to grin maniacally and deepened his voice to a rough contralto. " 'You got to know a lot about hard work. You got to have smelt a lot of mule manure before you can sing like a hillbilly. The people who has been raised the way a hillbilly has *knows* what he is singing about and appreciates it.' " Then Alvin would more than likely burst into tears, bow with dignity, and leave the room.

"Pagan idolater," Daddy would explain, matter-of-factly, to the horrified dinner guests, so that conversation could resume as usual.

"Alvin!" I yelled in my loudest, quiet whisper, "I'm *dying* in here." That got his attention all right, a face appeared with a nose strikingly lavender in shade.

"Business," said two purple lips, then the spectral-colored face returned outside, as though bent on picking up a few greens and indigo-reds. I noticed, in passing, that Alvin had the phonograph in his hands, was therefore in the process of doing Something Important, and so resolved at once to keep my mouth shut and my head under the bedcovers.

It might be noted here that our family lived, literally, out in the middle of nowhere. Our father, once a corporate lawyer in Atlanta, moved—with alacrity, he'd point out—kit and caboodle and new wife to Carter Valley, Tennessee, where he staked out several hundred acres and became a devout thinker-*cum*-vagrant-*cum*-teller of tall tales, and gentleman farmer. Mama, by virtue of having loved such a madman, did what she always does. She made do. And she made it well, single-handedly pulling what soon became a family of four through six lean, positively emaciated, years. Alvin and I, too, from the moment we could walk, pitched our efforts into the farm with a mighty gusto and an absolute lack of talent. To this day Mama remembers a manly two-year-old Alvin, half-drowned and surrounded by sorrowful thirsty cows, struggling valiantly out of a water trough he'd just filled.

The nearest city was Bull's Gap, ten miles away, a bustling little urban area approximately the size of a city block in Queens, containing, among a few other things, an elementary school, a hardware and farm equipment store, a Cas Walker grocery store, and eight extremely social Protestant churches, each of which slipped a phrase with "God" or "Jesus" or "Holy" into its title, boasted a congregation of at least a dozen, and chattily proselytized among the other churches for lack of an outside audience. "The Holy Icon Churches of God and Jesus His Son the Only Beleaguered Redeemer," Alvin called them, as well as "Those it-won't-hurt-a-bit salvation places."

The nearest house, though, was a ramshackle wooden structure only two hundred yards down the road and inhabited by a remarkably insane old woman, Miss Mildred. Above all else Miss Mildred loved to sit on her porch and take imaginary potshots at the appendages of unwitting trespassers against her, and she just sat there, decked out with a fine black silk dress, a string of cultured pearls, and a highly-polished and unloaded twelve-gauge shotgun, sat there all day long. Alvin, of course, was the only human being allowed inside her house, except that on certain occasions, when all winds and stars and shotguns were in collusion, I—that *other* young-un—would be allowed to sit, very quietly, on the porch, while they went inside and Miss Mildred taught Alvin how to play her big D28 Martin, a guitar mail-ordered, mysteriously, from Nashville. Sitting on that porch where Miss Mildred sat, with the Smoky Mountains just blue wisps in the distance, with Miss Mildred crying "Feeling now, boy, with *feeling!*" and Alvin strumming madly away with feeling, I felt, as I've rarely felt since, that the world was as beautiful and as serious, as perfect and complex and eminently handleable, as a highly-polished and forever unloaded twelve-gauge shotgun.

To return to that "out of the middle of nowhere" business; it's a lie. We were a family profoundly Somewhere, and we each of us clung like cornstalks to the soil and air and hills of East Tennessee. If we told stories or read stories aloud, we did so in our natural and unabashed hick idiom—sounds not excluding Shakespeare's "The Tamin of the Shrew" and "Much Do Bout Nothin"—because it *felt* right. If we fought like monkeys, and we did with real pleasure, if we fought and argued and picked at our faults in exacting detail, we did so because we *felt* like it and loved each other, not because we had ulterior motives or ulterior reasons or, Lord knows, exterior *goals*. We were honest-to-God, hoedowning, shitkicking, life-loving hillbillies, and we were smack in the middle of an overpowering somewhere.

To all irregionalists everywhere, to all mainstreaming, trend-following, media-addicted, suburban intellectual-mystic peoples everywhere, we ask you, from the bottom of our hearts, we ask you: From whence come *your* words?

Alvin once told me, on one of his more despairing days, that the essence of modern language and its slow death could be traced to a convalescent home in New Jersey, where the original movie

Tarzan was moved unceremoniously to a private suite because of his "repeated and disruptive elephant yells." We need every goddamn elephant yell we can get, he'd said, and we need them shoved into every available nook, cranny, and sphincter among us, he'd said. Alvin, even on his good days, was quite an elephant yeller himself. Sometimes you could hear his elephant yodel for miles and miles before he even opened his mouth.

When Richard Nixon was resigning in 1973, Alvin and I both happened to be home from our respective, if not wholly respected, northeastern colleges. We sat in the living room, ears poised toward the radio, and heard an ex-two-time president address the nation that voted for him and was listening to him for perhaps the last time. The muted flutter of the presidential helicopter sounded like static in the background. When he got to the part about Rose Kennedy, about how *his* mother would never have a biography written about *her* as Rose Kennedy had, Alvin jerked sharply upright, into his Lester Flatt G-run listening position. Then, when Nixon choked off the part about his mother and went tearfully on into the part about how the nation had to utilize and unify and rise ever onward over every obstacle, I looked up into Alvin's face. His eyes were teary, and Alvin's eyes, to the subjective observer, alternated between reflections of the sheerest sincerity and instruments of the most exposed torture. "He doesn't have the words, he doesn't have the *words*," he kept saying and sobbing, "Lord help us, we don't even have the *words* for our own goddamn tragedies!"

I woke up to find Alvin's pale blue face peering under the covers into my eyes. He might have been that Sam McGee from Tennessee in sore and poetic need of a healthy cremation. "Shut the *door*," I told him, as if he were intruding on a private conversation; I sleep the big sleep when I sleep. "Hug this," Alvin said. He then thrust under the covers what was effectively a frozen solid phonograph with an old Roy Acuff 78, "The Great Speckled Bird," iced over on top of it. Snow was melting rapidly, luxuriously, onto my green polka-dot percale sheets. "C'mon, warm it up," Alvin said. "Give it a hug." He bounced from the ball of one foot onto the other and back again, smacking his palms and smacking his lips, warming up, looking for all the world like a rabid football coach with an exotic skin disease. "Jesus damnit! Alvin," I cried, "it's going all over my bed!" "Right," he said enthusiastically. "Froze up on me, needs warmth."

When Alvin became enthusiastic there was nothing to do but relax and hug a frozen phonograph.

"That's the idea," he said. "Just hold on for a minute and I'll go downstairs and get the heating pad and be right back."

The heating pad in question was *the* heating pad, a 12- by 12-inch square of pink cotton material, flecked with maroon stars and stuffed with electrical circuits, used by our mother as a substitute bottle of aspirin, comforter of depressions, dryer of tears, and divine cure-all of endless childhood diseases. Once she nearly and lovingly suffocated Alvin during the treatment of a cold sore. Our father, on the other hand, who was never sick a day of his adult life—whenever either or both of us were "indisposed" (his word) by a violent case of measles or mumps—didn't know what the hell to make of us *or* the heating pad and generally retired to his ever-healthy cattle. One incident, though, does deserve mention. I remember Daddy entering my sickroom, on tiptoe no less, during a virulent case of chicken pox wherein even my tongue itched like fifty devils. "Thought you might like some entertainment," he had said, humbly, then he proceeded to read for seven uninterrupted hours the entire contents of Flannery O'Connor's *A Good Man Is Hard to Find*. Suffice it to say, he cured me of a great many things, except the chicken pox, during that session.

"Let's see what the story is," Alvin said, peeking under the blankets where the phonograph and I lay, arm to arm, in cold water. "Looking better," he said authoritatively, man-to-man with the phonograph. "Grippy, though, a little grippy." He all but took its pulse, lifting this, twirling that, sliding the record, blowing on the needle. At last he took it out and set it on the floor, plugged in the heating pad, and placed it gingerly over the phonograph.

"Wait see is what we do now," he told me, and nodded sagely. He sat cross-legged on the floor, a consoling hand on top of the heating pad, his eyes a troubled mixture of colors. Around the edges of his face there showed remnants of blue, but for the most part the skin had undergone a reversal, was pale, bloodless.

"Nothing personal, it ain't that," I said, "but what are you doing, Alvin?"

"I'm melting snow," said Alvin.

"I know, but what are you *doing?*" The water on my sheets was growing warmer by the minute, but it felt none too interesting.

"You know that verse in the Bible, that one that's the nine verse, twelve chapter somewhere?" I said, no, that I didn't, but that I would be very interested to hear it. "It went like this: 'Mine heritage is unto me as a speckled bird, the birds round about are against her.'"

Alvin could quote, at nine and at will, smidgens of songs, books, advertisements, movies, gossip, and even bird songs; he *attracted* all the good quotes.

"But that's Roy Acuff," I said. "That's that song right there, 'The Great Speckled Bird.'" I pointed elaborately in the direction of the heating pad.

"Bible did it first." He uncovered the phonograph for an experimental poke or two, then covered it back up. "Can't tell, though, who *really* said it, somebody just passing through. Heard it at the Church of God down to town."

"But what's it mean?" For all the cold air and open windows and wet sheets I was getting hot, hot and bothered. My brother was born with a knack, a sleight of imagination, for unconscious dramatic suspense, almost as though it might kill him, or kill something in him, if he ever got right to the point. I was getting hot and bothered.

"It's this bird," he explained. With the consoling hand he felt the phonograph, then screwed his face into a concentrated expression, considering its temperature. "Very better," he announced finally. Then slowly, painfully slowly, he unveiled the phonograph and after some cautious negotiation switched it on. Old Roy Acuff sang out with fuzzy, plaintive sincerity. His voice, at least, created no unsettling gusts of white air in the room; no cold words from old Roy.

"Business," said Alvin. He stood up and backed his way toward the window, phonograph in tow. Already the snow had drifted across the floor due to wind currents, although it had stopped snowing outside, and I stared blankly, fixedly, a veritable Robinson Crusoe in Nightgown, at Alvin's footprints on the floor. Alvin was back up on the sill, singing now, singing along with Roy Acuff.

"It's really weird to me," I said, grim as a soldier, "that whenever something important happens around here, I don't know what it is." Alvin reared back, teetering on the sill, and cast an appraising look in my direction.

"All right then," said Alvin. "Come on up and help me sing."

It was a hearty "Welcome Aboard" and I jumped out of bed, nightgown flapping, and joined Alvin on the catwalk of the sill. It was spectacularly cold up there, too cold for East Tennessee and so cold it might have been warmer than anything I'd ever known. Outside the moon shone forth in a sedate light and the snow, moon-silvered, had turned our farm to stone. The fenceposts around the cattle yard were entirely gone, disappeared, as though the very earth had surged upward to swallow all feeble boundaries. The cornfield, prickly with last year's stubble, was now a slab of solid marble. Through the trees that stood in funereal black procession across the back yard, I know I saw Jimmie Rodgers, thinner than a sapling, dancing with his Boston terrier, Mickey, prancing between the oaks of our farm. "Play that thing, boy!" he sang. And way off in the distance a single yellow square of light testified to a night of insomnia, of waiting and watching, at Miss Mildred's house.

"Don't be afraid," Alvin said. "Sing!"

In his eyes was the ecstatic glint of a madman, of someone very far away and irretrievably gone. So I sang, quietly at first, then louder, then louder still, until the world of stone outside cracked and gave way to country music. We sang in harmony, Roy and Alvin and I, and when Roy quit, Alvin started him up again. After an hour, though, hoarse and chilled, I said I'd had enough, that I'd give moral support from my bed but to bed I was going.

"Don't you want to know what we're doing?" Already in bed I said yes, yes, *yes* for goodness' sake.

"It's this bird," he said and pointed outside. I got out of bed and walked, rather impertinently, to the window.

"I don't see anything, Alvin, nothing. This isn't one of your games, is it? I want to know that right now. I want to know what's going on, it dark and cold and me not knowing what's going on. I'd like to know right now what's going on. It's *weird* is what it is." I had a good hold on Alvin's arm and jerked the sleeve of his pajamas for emphasis.

"Don't you see it? It's a bird down there." By leaning over the sill I could make out what looked like a black patent-leather woman's purse, spraddled messily on top of the snow.

"Is it alive?"

"Crippled," said Alvin.

"Why?"

"Flew into my window, never saw it, just flew around in the storm into my window and never saw it. Like a gunshot it sounded, like a snare drum." He paused, frowning, as if to remember how the lyrics went. "Then it crawled around the house over here and I figured maybe it could use some songs. Crippled itself and don't have no home it can go to. It'll be froze tomorrow and the others'll peck at it—that's the way birds do, peck and all."

I went back to bed and Alvin stayed put, singing. Before I fell asleep, in the back of my mind, I wondered whether a tear, dropped from a height of two stories in near-zero weather, wouldn't freeze before it hit the ground.

At sunrise Alvin woke me and told me to get dressed, we would go see the bird together. He hadn't slept and his eyes blazed, kindling some kind of desperate fever. In the back yard we crouched over the bird, didn't touch it; it was an ebony-glossed crow with one small speck of bright red blood on the yellow beak, and its legs stuck out rigidly to the side, like broken twigs. It certainly wasn't going anywhere anymore and I said as much and stood up, washing my hands of the whole business with a palmful of snow. Alvin, too, stood up. "Dead," he said sadly. "Old dead crow," he said, more sadly, then he smiled brightly, maniacally, and stamped his foot squarely onto the bird. It slid deep inside the snow and disappeared. He looked at me with that smile on his face. "I hope . . . " he began, but he never finished the sentence.

A special license of country music, and one I highly recommend, is the manipulation of anonymity. If not God, goes the

license, then by God *pretend* to be. Take that thing by its horns
and wrestle it, like St. Michael, to Kingdom Come and Back,
before it hits the newspapers. As Alvin said to me one rainy
Sunday morning, over the Bull's Gap *Review* comics section:
"You've got to sing the words for everybody, and if you leave
somebody out, you've got to make damn sure they'll at least hum
the tune for the rest of their life." He meant, I think, that the
country musician has to distill himself down to a cellular particle
approximately the size and shape of a human mouth in the act
of kissing Death.

With license in my back pocket, I accordingly whittle the past
from twenty years ago into a smaller, more compact, four. What
follows is not my story; it is, of course, my brother's. Before he
went gallivanting, with all utter seriousness, southward, he told
me this story in hiccupping, daily installments. Alvin was not
one for sordid detail, and even less for making points, drawing
conclusions, declaring an overt meaning, and his stories follow
the solid oral tradition of painless instruction. One is hit in the
head, repeatedly as a matter of fact, before one feels it, a
psychological effect closely akin to an aural placebo. What I'm
trying, awkwardly, to point out is for me the awful magnitude
of taking this particular thing by its particular horns and wrestling the particular life out of it.

The time, to be precise to the point of disinterest, will be exactly ten o'clock in the morning on May 18, 1976, and the young
man with the black beret, to be precise with considerably more
interest, will be my brother, twenty-five and traveling incognito.
As his sister and the stealer of his story, I interrupt here, or
better yet, I hereby *nip in the bud* the flow of this narration to say
one thing: I am a barefaced liar, as any member of my family,
and especially my brother, would be the first to admit; don't
trust me, and I mean it. Any lover of country music will understand this statement, will even forgive the self-consciousness of
this and any ensuing interruption, because soon, very soon, this
lover understands, the story must continue and, finally, end, regardless of my dishonesty—*in spite* of it, actually. For at the core
of any good country music lover beats the heart of a believer,
beats the heart of an inveterate truth seeker who, deep down,
believes that every word is at best a pack of decent lies and at

worst a matter of opinion, and that the real truth is in the melody. The *twang* so to speak, of the beloved.

Melissa: wherever you are out there, whatever you're doing, *I know you can hear this*. Listen.

One mugging, two pocket-pickings, and one attempted rape occurred during the young man's three-hour layover in the Washington Trailways station. He wore a black beret and carried a guitar case and had seen or overheard each of the four unrelated incidents with a facial expression of the keenest interest. Had it not been for his eyes—round, gray-brown, openly innocent eyes, the kind of eyes that are the confession of a whole face—but for those eyes he might have been mistaken for the gloating mastermind behind all four criminal acts. Nevertheless, as his eyes suggested, or rather, shouted, the young man with the black beret had merely been very interested: two days before in Port Authority he was robbed of every piece of luggage, every cent, and a carton of Marlboro cigarettes, by a roving lunatic with a switchblade. He had saved the guitar, though, telling the switchblade that, thank you, it would just have to kill him to get it and the switchblade, made a little awkward by the bulk of its spoils, had relented and rapidly withdrawn.

He stood on the boarding platform, guitar in hand, beret cocked like a trigger on the back of his head, and leaned in a quiet, neutral position against a concrete pillar. A decade before, he would have been a political caricature of himself, a stereotypic young man with a black beret, fresh, in the loose sense of the word, from New York. A decade before, he looked like the type of young man who might *give* everything he owned to a roving lunatic without a switchblade. Times change; no one looks like that any more. All decadent stereotypes had changed clothes, stiffened their upper lips, and risen ever onward toward the vicinity of Wall Street. Now they played their guitars for small social groups, cultivated interesting hobbies, met interesting people, and coolly observed the course of world and national affairs over green bottles of interesting bubbly-water. They were all very healthy in this decade, health apparently a first bastion of self-control, self-control apparently the sole bastion of utility. Any traveling young man with a black beret and a worn guitar was immediately suspect as a chic punk or a redneck who didn't know any better. This particular young man fell, plummeted, into the latter suspicion.

The young man coveted his health no more and no less than he trusted the weather. In fact he knew of at least nine latent cancers all over his body and yet he smoked, with relish, over a pack of cigarettes a day. He had jogged once, on impulse, down Fifth Avenue in order to skirt a group of small boys who were throwing water balloons at passersby. One, a blue one, hit him on the back of the head.

In truth he was not even from New York, had lived two years in a cat-infested fourth floor walk-up on East Seventh Street, which qualified him as an overstayed tourist in that city. Of the eight million possible accents there, his, he had felt, was the least acceptable. And although he tried to control it, temper it, beat it to death, the only surefire method of communication he'd hit upon was an extremely difficult maneuver, involving the placement of his tongue firmly against the inside of his cheek plus a sundry repertoire of hand gesticulations. In this manner, tiresome though it was, he might attempt the rudiments of accentless communication—hailing taxis, cashing checks, ordering food, "Please," "Thank you"—without hearing a "Whar you-all frahm, Sahnny?" In a Brooklyn accent. In a Brooklyn accent pleased as punch with itself and overcome with the pride of a voice that knows it can do a pretty good imitation or two. He had met each and every Italian, Jew, Dalmatian, high and low Bostonian, vegetarian, and Republican streetside mimic in New York City.

In this decade, however, he was headed home, to the Great State of Tennessee, and more particularly to Nashville where he would, without a doubt, become the greatest country music singer of his generation. Such were the ambitions of the times.

The express to Dallas, his connection, already hemmed and hawed at the gate, its unlit headlights staring at him, stupidly, right between the eyes. The bus reminded him, uncomfortably, of the cornbore caterpillars he used to mash on his family's farm. In thousands the caterpillars would devour sweet corn with a rapidity that seemed to come from an ugly grudge of a personal nature. An accident had occurred in his presence many years before. At an intersection called Bean Station, far from any town in East Tennessee, a tractor trailer rammed, almost nonchalantly, into a Greyhound bus. People flittered all over the pavement. And his only thought was: it looks like a caterpillar and they look like sweet corn. Afterwards, that very night, he went home and ate thirty-nine cornbore caterpillars, chewing well and swallowing; it had been only fair.

The young man accosted a rabid-looking man in fat trousers and asked for a cigarette, keeping an eye on the guitar in his hand as if it were a child, an unruly child that any minute might break free to inspect the gumball machines. The rabid man paused with a look of horror on his face, thrust an entire pack of cigarettes into the young man's hand, and muttered, "Missing my goddamn't bus, buddy," before waddling quickly on. Inside the man's mouth, he couldn't help noticing, only three yellow teeth had disrupted the empty symmetry. Briefly, but powerfully, the young man wanted to chase after the rabid man and pat his hollow cheek and maybe tell him a sadder story than the ones he already knew. Recently he had taken a turn for the worse, wanted to accost strangers in phone booths and shake their hands, wanted to attend the funerals of people he'd never known and weep, wanted to set the newspapers to music and sing of lives made black and white. He thought he might be crazy and almost, though not wholeheartedly, wished to hell he was. But deep down he knew he had never been saner.

"Thank you," he said, to no one in particular. By way of answer the sun rose over the metal horizon of the bus and blinded him for several seconds.

"Everbody get on board," said the driver to Dallas, in a surly baritone voice. The driver wielded, and wielded well, the impersonation of a bouncer in a hard-bitten country bar, intimating that he, by God, could take on any man boarding *his* bus. The sleeves of his regulation white shirt rolled back in neat creases above the elbow, clung tightly to the muscles there, and added a distinguished touch of elegance to the impression of scarcely suppressed violence. With a mouth wizened into distaste he assisted a woman and child up the steps by using their elbows as fulcrums and literally levering them into the bus. The young man scanned his ticket, a trifle desperately, to make sure all was without a doubt in order, and then handed it, rheumatically, over to the driver.

"What we got there," the driver said, grim as Death. His baritone was an instrument uniquely capable of rendering the shortest declarative sentence into a physical threat, and he stared with idle interest at the young man's ticket.

"I believe we've got a ticket," said the young man, grinning desperately. He had a sudden urge to explain in detail that he was just a conspicuous nitwit, passing through.

"Funny boy, huh." The driver glanced at him with a sweet grimace of introspection on his mouth. It was a short, indifferent once-over, as though he contemplated an open invitation to step back of the bus and discuss some things and maybe break somebody's neck.

"Nosir, honest to God, I haven't been funny for years." In a second, equally sudden urge, the young man wanted to point out that he was very likely the next Hank Williams and would probably need his body, in its entirety, in the near future.

"You know, funny boy," the driver said wistfully, "I could wipe that smile off four a you."

"I know, really, twenty, no kidding, thirty at least. I know you could do it, sir."

"All right then." With real finesse the driver hitched the sides of his trousers, like six-shooters, a little higher onto his waist. In the process he mutilated the young man's ticket. "We got luggage compartments for that'ere music."

"I know you do, I've known it for a hell of a long time, I can tell you that, sir. The thing is, this guitar and me, we're almost kin, that's the thing. You wouldn't put your sister under a bus, would you?"

The driver stared at him.

"I don't like you," he said, finally, with an impressive and ominous control. "Nor none of your kind, nor your hat neither. Get your butt on the bus, bud."

"Right," said the young man. "Will do. Bud on the bus right away." He leapt like a drowning man for the steps, stumbled on the second one, overturned a fire extinguisher with the guitar, then got back to his feet. A large knurl of chewing gum adhered to the side of the guitar case. "Bud's butt is on the bus," he told the gum, confidentially.

"Hey, funny boy." Down on the street the driver stood with his arm upraised; had he held a gun it would have been point-blank range. "Your ticket."

"Right," said the young man and he thrust out a hand that looked, strangely enough, like a branch in a gale-force wind. Into it the driver dropped a wad of paper approximately the size of a quarter.

"Thank you," the young man said.

"Just you sit in the back," said the driver with infinite patience, "or I might just lose my temper."

"Right," the young man agreed, "Way back, back to Methuselah."

Once the young man had seen Johnny Cash in concert, more live than life on the stage, and accompanied by June Carter who sang quite pleasantly at his left hand. During the refrain of "A Boy Named Sue" he was knocked unconscious from behind by an overexcited fan with a beer bottle just as Charlie Pride came onstage to join in on the fun. He had regretted that four-hour blackout ever since. Even now he felt a little faint, the recurrence of a possibly serious malady.

Down the aisle of the bus tier upon gray tier of inquisitorial faces watched him suspiciously as he negotiated himself and his guitar toward the rear. Those were the gray faces, he knew, that would form the juries of the future, that might follow the lead of yesteryear's decadent stereotypes and sentence the country to a status quo no longer handleable. Faceless and wordless they would sit and knit beside the guillotines of their own sons and daughters, fighting only for the right to front-row seats. And the hell of it was, a hell the young man had known from the day he picked up a guitar that belonged to a crazy old woman out in the middle of somewhere, the hell of it was that at the heart of every gray juror and every gray judge was a melody, as elusive as the character of America itself, and it was undeniably, ineradicably, a country melody of salvation. "For my next song," he wanted to say and wink engagingly at his audience, "something more on the upbeat side of things." Instead he proceeded, guitar foremost, toward the rear.

He passed, on his right, the woman and child who had been teeter-tottered into the bus, and he noticed that—although her magenta-colored hair was a little worse for wear and her pancake makeup had begun to scale off around the nose—the woman was lovely. The child sat primly on the seat next to the aisle, her little patent-leathered feet crossed neatly at the ankles, six inches above the floor, and her little lap obscured by a large unopened book entitled *Patterns of Grace*. She looked up and nodded officiously as he passed; he looked down and nodded officiously, if not zealously, back. Hers was the first unsolicited benign nod he'd received in two years.

He took the seats directly behind the woman and child, arranged his guitar with the care due an invalid on the plastic upholstery, then sat down beside the window. Outside the sun wreaked an interesting havoc on the neon signs of the strip joints across the street, and he lit a cigarette, observing that every man who entered a strip joint wore a polyester overcoat. He wondered whether polyester overcoats reflected a Washington style preference or whether they represented a secret rite of passage, like credit cards, into the realm of striptease. After a while the driver revved his bus into gear, gave a hearty deafening blast of the horn to several old men on the boarding platform (one of whom put a palm to his ear, as if he didn't quite catch the drift of the conversation), and they pulled out of the station, headed south.

The young man finished his cigarette and took out his guitar and, very quietly, began to fiddle around with a few bars of a new tune. For weeks he'd been working on it, refining it, wrestling with it, but something—maybe only a chord or two—was missing. In all honesty, he wanted this tune to sound like nothing short of an elephant giving birth to the continent of Africa, without an anesthetic.

"You need to go from D to A in eighth notes," said a high-pitched voice. It was the child or, rather, the child's head, propped on the seat in front of him. And it was, in fact, exactly what he needed to do. The young man jerked sharply upright.

"How do you know that?"

Invitation enough, the child climbed over, not around, her seat, and settled demurely into the seat beside the young man.

She crossed her legs. She rubbed her nose, delicately, as only the polite veteran of many runny noses can do. She adjusted her hair ribbon that held her medium-length red hair in token control. In short, she took her own sweet time.

"I don't believe we've been introduced," she said and extended her left hand.

The young man apologized profusely, shook her hand vigorously, and said that his name was Bud, that he'd come from New York, and that he was headed for Nashville.

"My name is Melissa," she said. "You may call me Melissa. My mother's name is also Melissa, but she's asleep. Buses give her the morning sickness. My father was an unknown factor really." She looked to her right, craned her neck behind them, ascertained that the coast, as it were, was clear and continued, *sotto voce*: "You may have noticed that I'm a genius. At the present moment I am disguised as a perfectly normal eleven-year-old child, but I'm really twenty-two. I've been tested. Five times. I would appreciate your silence." She directed a penetrating look, with eyes no larger than dimes, toward the young man who promptly assured her that, as far as he was concerned, mum was the word.

"You're not, I hope, a *pop*ular singer?" She stressed the word "popular" with an unmistakable, but very pretty, groan. Then she asked for a cigarette and recrossed her legs. When the young man suggested, solicitously, that perhaps a cigarette would be bad for her health, Melissa gave a much less pretty groan and produced, from her back pocket, a pack of Marlboro cigarettes. The young man lit her cigarette, not out of courtesy, but because he was becoming, more or less, quite afraid of her.

"My life expectancy," she said, inhaling, "is endless really. Are you a popular singer?"

The young man said, no, he was not, that he played country music, a genre in itself unpopular in most areas, that he had yet to make his mark even in an unpopular genre, and that, in effect, he was absolutely unknown except to blood relatives and an occasional stranger.

"Good," said Melissa. "You should go to Central America then."

He readily agreed, would have agreed at this point to go almost anywhere she saw fit to tell him to go, then, come to think of it, he asked: "Why?" She cast an appraising look at him, rubbed her nose, and settled more comfortably against her seat. She blew out a perfect ring of smoke and watched it float off toward the front of the bus.

"You'll have to learn Spanish," she decided. "And you'll have to travel light. Do you speak Spanish? I'm fluent really, know around four hundred and thirty-three words, not including numbers. Any child could do the numbers."

"But why," said the young man, "should I go to Central America?" In his excitement he burned his elbow on the cigarette Melissa held in her left hand.

After a flurry of apologies, mostly from the young man, Melissa sighed and leaned forward. "Because," she said. "It needs to be heard. I'm going there myself, when I come of age. That'll be in about seventy-two months."

At this she stubbed out her cigarette and stood up, explaining that her mother disliked to wake up alone. Her mother was the "clinging type," she said, "and worried about every little thing," whereupon she performed a curtsy, on top of the seat, and climbed over the ramparts to where her mother slept. For the rest of the day and all night she didn't say another word to the young man.

Early the next morning he woke to the smell of coffee and, squinting his eyes, found Melissa in the seat beside him; she sat there and read her book and held a Styrofoam cup of coffee in one hand. From the vantage point of eyes that were supposed to be asleep, he tried to size her up, to make sense out of her, to see what she could possibly be. It turned out that she looked like an eleven-year-old child reading a book and drinking a cup of coffee.

"Quit looking at me," she said. "It just so happens that my mother makes snores and this is the only available seat on the whole bus. I thought you could be trusted, that's all. We're almost to Nashville, you know, and I slept very badly. Everybody used up all the air. I'm fit to be tied really."

"Good morning," said the young man. He, too, had slept badly, had not slept well for longer than he cared to remember. It struck him that everybody had been using up his air for quite a while.

"It's a terrible morning," Melissa said. She closed her book.

"It's raining and the newspapers at the rest stop said our president fell down again. Off a *plane*. In front of a million cameras. Those men are always falling down somewhere in front of a camera. It's a terrible morning really. Would you care for some coffee?"

"Thank you, yes." The young man took off his beret and placed it in his lap, attempting against all odds to look presentable. Among other things, he was unshaven, unwashed, penniless, unhappy, and fairly uncertain. Things, however, were looking brighter. Melissa exchanged the coffee for the beret, which she placed on top of her head.

"Do you think I'm cute?" she asked, coyly. The young man pointed out that cute was really an understatement.

"My mother was beautiful in her prime. She was a professional woman. We're going to Dallas, Texas, to further her career. She dances, badly enough, but Uncle Burnt—he's her manager, insists I call him Uncle but he isn't really, looks more like a massive murderer to tell the truth—Uncle Burnt says they may not know the difference in Dallas." Melissa took off the beret, punched it several times, stretched it out, punched it again, then returned it to the young man's lap. "I'm one of those bittered children," she said and sighed. "It's made me very religious though. I was an immaculate birth, you know. I'm practicing to be a martyr, but once I punched this girl, Marcia Dinwiddie, in the face for making a sinuous comment on my mother, so I might be disqualified already. Do you believe?"

"In what?" the young man asked. In five minutes he had progressed from a fitful sleep to the very edge of his seat. "I mean believe in what?"

"You do," Melissa said, "I can see you do. Your eyes are a dead giveaway really. I collect eyes, matched pairs only. Once I met this woman that had one green eye and one blue one. Honestly. But what happened was, she used contacts. She *wanted* two different eyes. I really couldn't see that."

The young man nodded. He said he really couldn't see that, either, then he asked her where she came from. He still sat, perched like a pigeon, on the edge of his seat.

"I was born in Okemah, Oklahoma, you know, where that guy Woody Guthrie came from, but I'm pretty flexible. I was only a very young baby then." She paused, rubbing her nose with a poised index finger. "It's not where anyway, it's how. I learned music in Tampa Bay, Florida, and got a sunburn and went to a hospital. I learned Spanish from this man with a finger where his thumb was supposed to be, out in Dracula, Georgia. I had a boyfriend in Washington, D.C., where they tested me for the I.Q., but we left there and I was glad. He had these nitwit canaries at his house and every time you went there he'd go up to those canaries and say 'How are we today?' like he was a canary too, or like they weren't doing terrible in that nitwit cage. Then his mother would come in, she's why I was glad we left, and *she'd* ask them how they were, too, and make us come over and look at them sing. At night they put a blanket over it to shut them up. They were all nitwits, especially the birds. He was my only boyfriend. I adored him a little bit really."

Melissa pulled reflectively on the hem of her skirt.

"I have to be running along," she said. "She'll wake up any minute. She's a very nervous person when she wakes up on buses." She stood up with her book. The young man stood up, awkwardly, one knee on the seat, and said he hoped they'd meet again.

"It's likely," she said, "I get around. Do you ever write unquieted love songs, because if you do, I'll keep my ears open." With her free hand she placed a finger beside her nose, looking up at the young man. "Do you think you could kiss my forehead goodbye?" she asked pensively. "Just a little one, really, is all I want." The young man complied with no hesitation whatsoever, and kissed the place a half an inch below the part of Melissa's hair.

It happened right then, and it happened quickly. First, not two feet away, came an incredibly high-pitched, resounding scream that listed sideways and echoed down the aisle of the bus like a tidal surge. Every face turned around and the bus pulled over to the side of the road. Next, Melissa disappeared and a torsoless head of magenta-colored hair began to bob up and down, screaming "Rape! Rape!" in a voice that, unbelievably, didn't shatter every glass object in a three-mile radius. The young man grabbed hold of his guitar, as if it might prove to be an anchor through the ground swell. It did not. In his approach the driver to Dallas rolled up his shirtsleeves and, upon arrival in the rear, picked the young man bodily from his seat by the scruff of the neck, carried him effortlessly, guitar and all, back down the aisle, and tossed him like so much chaff out the door and into the street.

"Preverted motherfucker!" the driver yelled, then he slammed the door shut. Forty faces peered with obvious delight out of six large windows.

The young man picked himself up slowly. He executed a quick double check, found himself to be intact, in his entirety, and found his guitar to be roughed up, though healthy. He watched his connection to Nashville disappear around a stand of forlorn pine trees. And then, for reasons uncertain, but certainly for questions unanswered, he began to sprint at a high speed down the road, through the rain, after the bus, into the direction of Dallas, Texas; he was going to follow her, find her—grab on to her, cleave to her—listen to her, ask her—

There is a second license of country music, one often confused for a very different thing, and it concerns the nature of sentimentality. I shall dispose of this matter right now. Back in the thirties when Roy Acuff first recorded, a story floated around asserting that whenever he sang a sad song he wept openly because of a "sentimental" nature; it's a lie. Sentimentality is rose-colored and walks a poodle. What Roy Acuff saw and felt and sang was a different color, and sadder than even a poodle. The second license of country music is, of course, sentimentality standing precariously upon its head. It is a view of the world from the bottom up, blood rushing toward the brain, arms trembling, feet flailing. It wants more than anything in the world to see things right-side up, and it's scared to death it will.

After my brother's death they shipped the guitar with him by steamer and by freight train back home to Carter Valley. He died in Nicaragua, guitar in hand, with a well-aimed sniper's bullet in his head. He died there, for unspeakably good reasons, two years ago. I happen to have his guitar with me, and although I can't play it, still I can sit, very quietly, and look out over the frozen Hudson River, and then I can hear the thing for miles and miles.

Melissa, wherever you are out there, whatever you're doing, I *know* you can hear it, too: Listen—